"You want to trade four dozen eggs for one pie?" Raif argued.

"The pie is worth it! Being an obvious out-of-towner, you haven't tasted my aunt's pies," observed Heather. "Her Key Lime Fluff is the talk of Mimosa, Florida."

"A man could sell his soul for less," Raif admitted.

And a man with a smile like that should be outlawed, Heather thought. "Let me have the eggs right now, and I'll bring you a sample tomorrow. Deal?"

He took a step closer to her. "That's asking a lot."

They were nose to nose, and being so close to this man didn't do much for keeping a clear head. She could step back, but that would give him a psychological advantage—or so she'd read in one of those assertiveness-training books.

Raif ran a practiced eye over Heather's trim figure. He approved of her piquant looks and knockout legs. And she wasn't bad when it came to negotiating a deal, either.

He was definitely going to enjoy his vacation on his friend's chicken farm . . . because he was really going to enjoy getting to know this woman.

Dear Reader,

Welcome to Silhouette Romance—experience the magic of the wonderful world where two people fall in love. Meet heroines who will make you cheer for their happiness, and heroes (be they the boy next door or a handsome, mysterious stranger) who will win your heart. Silhouette Romance reflects the magic of love—sweeping you away with books that will make you laugh and cry; heartwarming, poignant stories that will move you time and time again.

In the next few months, we're publishing romances by many of your all-time favorites such as Diana Palmer, Brittany Young, Annette Broadrick and many others. Your response to these authors and others in Silhouette Romance has served as a touchstone for us, and we're pleased to bring you more books with Silhouette's distinctive medley of charm, wit and—above all—*romance*.

During 1991, we have many special events planned. Don't miss our WRITTEN IN THE STARS series. Each month in 1991, we're proud to present you with a book that focuses on the hero—and his astrological sign.

I hope you'll enjoy this book and all of the stories to come. Come home to romance—Silhouette Romance—for always!

Sincerely,

Tara Gavin
Senior Editor

SHARON FRANCIS

Hot Time

Silhouette Romance

Published by Silhouette Books New York

America's Publisher of Contemporary Romance

For Bee and Irv Harrington,
Dorothy and Don Ward,
and all the chickens.

SILHOUETTE BOOKS
300 E. 42nd St., New York, N.Y. 10017

HOT TIME

ISBN: 0-373-08769-1

First Silhouette Books printing January 1991

Printed in the U.S.A.

SHARON FRANCIS

was fourteen years old when she was first published—her short story appeared in an English teen magazine—and she has been writing ever since. Currently, she has over twenty published titles to her credit, including several young-adult novels. A former English teacher, Sharon makes her home with her husband in Massachusetts, where they've raised two grown sons and where she's a columnist for a local paper and a teacher of writing.

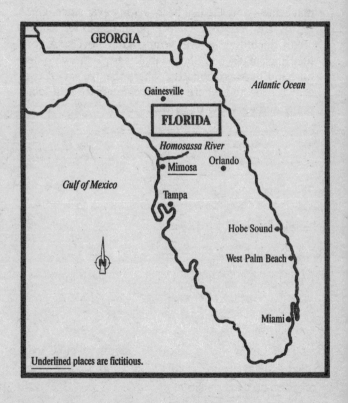

GEORGIA

Atlantic Ocean

Gainesville

FLORIDA

Homosassa River

Orlando

Mimosa

Gulf of Mexico

Tampa

Hobe Sound

West Palm Beach

Miami

Underlined places are fictitious.

Chapter One

Someone was strumming a ukelele nearby, and the swish of the hula girls' grass skirts stroked the sun-kissed air. Raif leaned back in his deck chair, reached for a cool one, then stopped to frown. That shrill whining sound didn't fit the mood.

Nevertheless the noise continued. It sounded like—dammit, it *was* the telephone. Reluctantly, Raif opened his eyes.

It was pitch dark. Disorientation hit him until he realized that he was in his office. His swivel chair was tilted back at an impossible angle, and his feet were propped up on the rosewood desk.

Earlier that day he had drawn the drapes to cut down on the sun's glare. That sun had long gone, and so had everyone else. He'd dismissed his staff and urged Joan, his faithful secretary, to go home on time for once. Then he himself had settled down to wait for a phone call from Ted Kovacheck.

Joan had typed up his notes on today's visit to Raifoods' Westwood plant, and he'd been going over them when he closed his eyes. Now, his watch put the time at seven. He swung his long legs off the desk, reached for the phone receiver and asked, "Everything all right?"

"Couldn't be better, Raiford," the enthusiastic voice boomed back. "How's every little thing with you?"

It certainly wasn't Kovacheck. Raif shook his head clear of sleep and muttered, "Ah, George?"

"Right in one, Raiford," the loud voice on the other end informed him. "In case you haven't figured it out, it's January again. So, am I going to see you this year or not?"

The last time Raif had seen his former roommate and fraternity brother had been eight years ago at George's wedding. He had a sudden memory of himself as best man trying to calm George, whose six-foot-four, two-hundred-and-eighty-pound frame had been quivering with nerves.

"Are you calling from Florida?" he asked.

"From Mimosa, Florida, otherwise known as God's country. And it's here waiting for you, Raiford."

For the past eight years, George had called off and on extending the invitation to come to visit him. Raif had no idea where Mimosa was except that it was someplace in west central Florida. George had moved there after marrying Carolann Titus, a Florida girl whom he'd met at Boston University. Raif always meant to visit George and Carolann someday, but there was never enough time.

"And don't give me the same 'I'm too busy with Raifords' line," George lectured. "Let me tell you, old son, this is the life. Today while you suckers shoveled out from under the latest blizzard, I walked around in shorts. It was eighty degrees warm when I drove over to the pier and dropped in a line. Two seconds later, I pulled out my first trout." He paused to add, "Bet it's snowing where you are."

Raif glanced at the window. Through a gap between the drapes, he could see that there were indeed white objects floating through the darkness.

"It's unnatural living in that climate," George said sadly. "I put that to your father once, God rest him. I said, 'Mr. Cornell, the reason why you Bostonians are so uptight is that you work too damn hard. And why do you work so hard? Because you can't stand to leave your temperature-controlled office and face the weather outside.' Know what he said?"

"I can guess." Raif grinned reminiscently. "Dad was the kind of guy who took the Yankee work ethic personally."

A rich chuckle wafted across the lines. "Well, I'd say the apple hasn't fallen far from the tree. Now that you've made Fortune 500, though, you should be good to yourself. What're you doing at the office at this hour?"

Raif glanced down at his desk, which was covered with the reports, analyses and figures pertaining to his latest acquisition.

"I'm waiting for a phone call," he explained.

"After which you'll work till midnight. What you need is to come down to Mimosa and put up your feet."

There was a faint splattering sound. Even through the expensive thermopanes, Raif could hear the wind-driven snow. It made him feel even more weary than he already was. "You know, I wish I could."

"What's stopping you? Delegate Raifoods to your underlings, have your secretary call for reservations and pack your cutoffs and a pair of sneakers." George added, "Be good to yourself for once."

For an instant Raif allowed himself to picture a warm golden sun, a life that was free of corporate meetings and fiscal reports, an existence where time was measured not in work or in boring New Year parties but in sunshine and relaxation. The picture was tantalizing. And he'd promised himself a vacation as soon as the Swiftee deal went down.

He sighed with genuine regret. "It's not that easy."

George shifted gears. "I've been thinking about you a lot lately, old son. After I read that article about you in that business magazine, I got to reminiscing. Remember the day we 'redecorated' the field after that game with B.C.? And there was the time we got Bob Ormsteader smashed and left him in the middle of the chapel with a lily on his chest." As Raif laughed, George added wickedly, "Then there was the night you made a date with Carolann *and* Lily Petrie at one and the same time."

Raif's green eyes narrowed. "Listen, you set me up. You wanted Carolann to think me a louse so you could move in. I only forgive you because you asked me to be your best man." He paused. "How is Carolann?"

A gusty sigh shook the connecting wires. "Gone, Raiford. Our marriage folded last summer." Another sigh. "She moved to Miami and I hear she's dating a nerdy insurance type now."

Raif could think of nothing to say but, "Aha."

"The trouble started after I left Stanton Foggarty and started out on my own. And how about you? Been too busy making money to tie the knot, hey? Maybe some pretty little Yankee is holding you back from coming down and watching those trout skipping around in the water. I read someplace that you were romancing Senator Hardy's daughter. Anything come of it?"

For someone buried in the backwaters of Florida, George was well informed. "As it happens, no."

"Well, don't fret, old son, there are plenty of fish in the sea. Southern girls will bring the old sparkle back in your eye. When are you flying down?"

The call-waiting beep had begun to sound in Raif's ear. He switched the connection and heard Ted Kovacheck's gravelly voice rasp, "Sorry I've kept you waiting, boss."

"Hang on a minute, Ted." Raif switched the connection again and found George talking to himself. "I hate to go, George, but the call I've been waiting for came in. I'll get back to you."

He switched again and Kovacheck said, "The meeting with Swiftee's attorneys ran overtime, Raif. That's why I'm late."

Raif frowned, and a knot of tension began to beat against his temple. Ted and he had fine-combed the contract that would bring Swiftee's fast-food chain under Raifoods' aegis, but there could have been unforeseen problems. "Talk to me, Ted," he said.

"You know how it is. The smallest wrinkles are the hardest to iron out. But it should run smoothly from now on, believe me."

Kovacheck's growl carried satisfaction, and Raif relaxed. He trusted Ted's instincts as well as his knowledge of corporate law. Kovacheck had been his late father's attorney and right-hand man when the senior Cornell started Raifoods. Now he headed Raif's legal department.

Back in those days Raifoods had been a small frozen-food line. Now, largely because of Raif's vision and modern concepts of marketing gourmet frozen foods, the company was giving established firms serious competition. Now Raifoods was expanding its New Jersey market by acquiring Swiftee, a Newark-based food processing firm.

The Swiftee acquisition had occupied much of his working time for the past few months. "I owe you a steak dinner," he told Ted.

Raif replaced the receiver in its cradle, stretched his lean, hard-muscled body to its full six foot one, then strode across the room for his overcoat. Outside in the corridor, he nodded to the fifty-third-floor security man. "'Night, Harry."

"G'night, Mr. Cornell. Drive carefully, now. It's snowing like a son of a gun outside."

By the time he reached the lower level parking garage, this fact had become painfully apparent. Though protected from the elements outside, the garage was bitterly cold. Raif thought of George Montfort's remarks about Boston weather as he drove his car outside onto State Street.

Usually he walked or jogged the half hour's journey to his Joy Street town house. Today, because he'd had to inspect the plant in Westwood, he'd brought his car. Raif regretted this move as snow hurled itself at his window. To make matters worse, there was a traffic jam near Quincy Market, and Cambridge Street was like a parking lot. Raif inched his car forward, then winced as the front left wheel lurched into a hidden pothole. A few minutes later he knew he had a flat tire.

Raif pulled to the side of the road and got out. Windblown snow made it hard to see, and as he was reaching for his jack, a truck came careening by and missed him by inches.

"Hey!" Raif shouted. "Watch where you're going, idiot!"

Another car roared up, hit a puddle the size of Lake Ontario and doused Raif with muddy water. He swore long and fervently and in midcurse thought again of golden sun, fresh-caught trout and an old friend he hadn't seen in years.

The vision held him until he realized snow was trickling down the back of his neck. Paradise was very far away. Grimly, Raif pulled up the collar of his soaking coat and began to replace the tire.

* * *

The old girl was preparing to die. Heather could hear her wheeze as she crawled up the slight incline.

"You can do it, Mehitabel," she coaxed.

The pickup clanked mournfully, and her gears gave out an awful, grinding whine. It had been badly neglected since Sam passed away last spring. Maggie drove her old station wagon, so she wouldn't have thought to take Mehitabel in for routine maintenance. Besides, it might have been too painful for Maggie to go to the Big S Garage now that Eddy Simms, once Sam's chief mechanic, owned the place. It would be one more reminder that Sam was gone, and—

"Oh, rats," Heather exclaimed. She'd missed the turnoff to the chicken farm again.

Actually, she'd missed it three times. Three times she'd driven up and down the length of winding White Hill Road without spotting the side street that would lead her to Mountain Farm. Slowing Mehitabel to a crawl, Heather tried again. The road *had* to be somewhere around.

While she had been living in New York, she had thought often of her hometown. She'd missed the days of sparkling sun and the gorgeous gulf sunsets and the tranquil nights. She had also forgotten how underdeveloped some areas of Mimosa still were. Those groves of scrubby pine, palmetto and tangled brush offered no hint of civilization—or of a road.

"There it is!" Heather shouted.

To the right of her was a narrow trail leading up an incline, and on a pine tree was a sign that read Moun-

tain Farm. It was faded and hung lopsidedly from a
solitary nail. No wonder she had missed seeing it,
Heather thought.

She coaxed Mehitabel onto the rutted path, and the
ancient pickup groaned as it climbed the slope. "Don't
you dare give up now," Heather pleaded, but halfway
up the incline Mehitabel stopped. Heather climbed out
of the driver's seat, pulled a screwdriver out of her
shirt pocket and lifted the hood. A cloud of steam
drove her back.

In frustration she ran a hand through her thick
brown curls. "Overheating in January," she groaned.
"Mehitabel, how could you?"

She hadn't brought any water with her, but there
were two empty milk jugs in the back. Heather replaced the screwdriver in her pocket, hoisted her
leather pocketbook over her shoulder and picked up
the containers. Then she started walking toward
Mountain Farm.

In spite of the fact that the dirt road was rocky,
pockmarked with holes and hard to negotiate, she
walked briskly, and by the time she reached the top of
the slope she was wishing she'd worn shorts instead of
a plaid shirt and jeans. Reminding herself that New
Yorkers would kill for such weather, Heather set down
the containers, removed the scarf she'd tied around
her neck and wiped her forehead with it. Then she
looked down at Mountain Farm.

It had been built into a hollow that might charita-
bly be described as a valley. It wasn't a big farm, nor
did it look particularly prosperous, boasting only one
hopper and a large, squat, well-ventilated wooden

structure that was probably the laying house. A wire-mesh fence surrounded this building, and a few chickens were strutting and pecking there. A little apart, crowded by scraggy pines and pepper trees, stood a small farmhouse.

At least she had come to the right place. Heather pushed the scarf into her jeans pocket and picked up her milk jugs again. Now, all she had to do was find the owner of the farm, and—

She started as a white rooster came rearing out of the underbrush. It was a big bird with a bright red comb and wattles, and it had a mean-looking beak through which it made rasping sounds. The bird's neck feathers were puffed, its russet eyes angry. The spurs on its legs looked like bayonets.

Remembering her 4-H training, Heather made soothing sounds. Not soothing enough, apparently, for the rooster flew at her. Instinctively, Heather used the milk containers as a shield, but the shock of the bird's attack knocked them out of her hands.

Swinging her pocketbook, she retreated. "Get away from me, you varmint! What did I ever do to you?"

Heather yelped as its spurs punctured her pocket-book. Next moment, it had retracted its weapons and hopped back out of reach. From the looks of things, it was getting ready to attack again. Refusing to give in to a cowardly impulse to run for her life, Heather tugged her scarf out of her pocket. If she could just use it to hood the bird's eyes . . .

There was a shout in the near distance, and she saw a tall, dark-haired man racing toward her. She'd just registered the fact that he moved with the clean, even stride of an athlete when the rooster jumped her again.

She tried to drape her scarf over its head, but she didn't move quickly enough, and one of the rooster's spurs made contact with her calf. Heather was yelling her pain when the dark-haired man reached her and made a grab at the bird.

"Watch for its spurs," Heather shouted.

Too late. The man's bellow was impressive. Then he went down into a football crouch and tackled the rooster. There was a loud squawking, a flurry of feathers and several choice expletives.

"Hold still, you miserable bird," Heather's rescuer growled.

He was holding the rooster like a football. Undaunted, the bird attempted to spear its enemy with its beak. Heather picked up her scarf from the ground and limped forward.

"Keep clear. What do you think you're going to do with that thing?" the dark-haired man demanded.

"I'm going to hood his eyes. Once he can't see, he'll calm down." She hesitated, intimidated by the furious russet eyes and wicked beak. "Ah, if you'll hold the back of his neck? Gently, or you'll hurt him."

"Did you say hurt *him?*" One dark eyebrow had slanted up and green eyes examined her as though she were demented.

Heather managed to drape the scarf over the rooster's eyes. As the fowl began to turn his head about in a helpless way she added, "He should simmer down now."

"What made him attack you in the first place?" the man wondered.

His eyes were really green, Heather thought. Almost as green as new spring leaves, they dominated a lean, square-jawed face. Heather guessed he hadn't seen the sun for months, for his hard-planed cheeks and his bold nose were pink with sunburn.

His accent was wrong, too. Though Florida had become a melting pot of snowbirds from all over the country, this man's words were delivered in the crisp manner of someone used to issuing orders. He looked as though he were slumming in his faded cutoffs, T-shirt and dilapidated sneakers. He was, Heather decided, the strangest chicken farmer she'd ever seen.

"I suppose he thought I was going to hurt him," she replied. Then she asked, "Do you own Mountain Farm?"

The tall man shuddered visibly. "God, no."

Curioser and curioser, Heather thought. Aloud she asked, "Then who's responsible here?"

The question made him frown. "I suppose I am, temporarily. I apologize for this bird. He must've gotten out through one of the torn places in the fence." The deep voice altered as he asked, "Did he hurt you?"

There was a red-rimmed hole in her jeans. Gingerly Heather rolled up her pants leg and poked experimentally at the puncture mark in her calf. "I think he made contact."

"I *am* sorry. He got me a couple of times, too. Those damn spurs are like bayonets! If you'll come to the house, I'll get some antiseptic ointment. No telling how many germs our friend carries around with him."

Heather glanced doubtfully at the still-irate rooster. "Actually," she began, "I came to ask you—" But the dark-haired man was already striding away.

There was nothing she could do but limp after him. She watched him open the wire gate of the compound and dump the rooster inside, then bend to retrieve a fishing rod that he'd thrown down by the side of the road. Apparently he'd been fishing instead of mending fences.

"Won't he get out again?" Heather wondered.

He shook his head. "George plugged up all the holes this morning after a few dozen of his hens escaped and had to be rounded up. I helped him, but I guess we missed our friend in the general confusion."

"It sounds like a scene from an escape movie," Heather couldn't help murmuring.

"And you got caught in the shoot-out." His grin was wry, directed as much at himself as at her. Heather couldn't resist the smile in his green eyes.

"I'll live. Now, the reason I came here, Mr...."

"Raif Cornell. Please call me Raif."

She said, "Heather Leigh," and held out her hand.

Raif approved of Heather Leigh's hand. It was slender, long fingered and very capable. Any work that was left in such hands would get done. And the rest of her was good to look at—dark-lashed hazel eyes, a mouth that was cut a little too wide for beauty but perfect for smiling, freckle-dusted peach-bloom skin, which stretched over good bones. A cap of flyaway brown curls crowned some five feet six inches of long-legged, gently curved slenderness.

And she had a pleasant voice, slightly husky and easy on the ear with its mere suggestion of a southern drawl. Raif realized she was saying something about pies and eggs.

"Is that possible?" she asked.

Having no clue as to what she'd been talking about, Raif hedged. "Anything's possible. Let's see about your wound first, though. The house is this way."

Even while he was speaking, he recalled the condition of the house. He'd meant to clean up this morning, but had gone fishing instead. After the blizzard he'd left behind him in Boston, the warm, golden sun and the thought of fish jumping had been too good to resist.

After hastily striding up the stairs ahead of her, he propped his fishing rod by the screen door and scooped up empty beer cans, several back issues of an outdoors magazine and a pair of dirty sneakers from a chipped wooden rocker.

"It's not much on looks but it's sturdy," he reassured her. "Sit down, and I'll go find the first aid kit."

Heather had never beheld a more pitiful mess than the inside of this farmhouse. Through the patched screen windows she could see clothes strewn everywhere, books, magazines, fishing tackle and beer cans resting on chairs and tables and stacked on the floor. A Norman Rockwell print on the wall was tilted at a crazy angle, and a black-and-white photograph of Groucho Marx leered at her over his cigar.

Before she could wonder how any ten people could be such slobs, Raif was back with a first aid kit and a large bottle of rubbing alcohol. He knelt at her feet and began swabbing her leg with alcohol. She stifled a yelp as the cool liquid hit her torn flesh.

"I'm sorry if this hurts." He worked with a sureness that was totally out of keeping with the rest of the farm. She was wondering about that when he said, "You'll probably need a tetanus booster. So will I, come to think of it. Is there a clinic around here?"

If he didn't know that old Doc Zermer was the only game in town, he definitely had to be a newcomer to Mimosa. She gave him directions, then added, "How long have you been in charge of Mountain Farm?"

"I'm not," he replied.

Intrigued, Heather waited for him to continue, but before he could, an alarm clock went off.

"Pay no attention to that," Raif said. "George is absentminded, so he sets the alarm at chow time." He saw Heather looking bewildered, and explained, "For the barnyard crew, I mean. The alarm is set to remind George that the timer is going to open the hopper and turn on the food-conveyor belt."

During her 4-H days she'd learned a lot about how chickens were fed and cared for. "But why would you need an alarm for that?" she wondered. "And who is George?"

"My college roommate and fraternity brother. He invited me down for a holiday." Raif applied ointment to Heather's shapely calf and tried to keep his mind on what he was saying. "George was a business major at B.U., and he thought it would be profitable to go into chicken farming. He originally wanted to breed chickens, and got several roosters like the one that attacked you. But then he changed his mind and decided to specialize in eggs."

His fingers stroked on more ointment. His touch shouldn't have been disconcerting, but it was. Heather did her best to ignore the odd sensations that were spreading up her injured limb and seeping through to the rest of her.

"Where is your friend now?" she asked.

"In town picking up supplies. He should be back soon, and—"

A loud buzzer sounded and a red light over the porch door began to flash. Alarmed, Heather watched Raif leap to his feet, vault over the porch railing and tear toward the laying house.

The buzzer continued to bleep furiously as Raif threw open the door of the laying house and ran inside. Was the man crazy, or was the farm about to self-destruct? Determined to find out, Heather limped down the steps after him.

She found him dumping empty buckets under an ancient food-conveyor belt. The belt had stopped moving, but the hopper was still disgorging food. The feed had already piled onto the motionless food belt and was spilling onto the ground.

"Do you know what to do?" she asked.

He shook his head. "George didn't tell me, damn him."

There was a control box near the mouth of the pipe that led from the hopper to the conveyor belt. "Suppose you pull that switch," Heather suggested. "It should shut everything down."

Raif complied, and the machinery whirred to a stop. "George's equipment's old," he said, "and it's given him trouble before. That's the reason for all those alarms and buzzers. He told me he'd rigged them to alert him for possible trouble." He hopefully eyed the overflowing conveyor belt. "Supposing I leave everything shut down?"

Heather shook her head. "If they're not fed for more than a few hours, chickens go into molt and stop laying."

"George will be home long before that," Raif began, then remembered that George had never been on time for anything in his life. He'd probably stop downtown to have a cool one, maybe get into a game of pool. "I suppose I'd better call a repairman," he said.

"I doubt if you could get anyone. Percy Reubens runs the only repair shop in town and he's usually on the road around this time of day." Heather stood on tiptoe to examine the wiring inside the control box. "It may just be a case of the timer getting messed up. If I cleaned the relays, that might do it."

He eyed her with new respect. "Do you clean relays?"

They were standing very close together. When Raif moved, she could feel the hair on his arm brush her skin. Heather registered that oddly provocative shadow touch while saying, "I can, but I'll need my pocketbook."

He didn't stop to question her but was off at a run. Seconds later, he handed her the pocketbook so that she could search for an emery board. "To scrape down the relays," she explained.

He kicked over an upended bucket. "Best stand on this."

He watched her closely as she cleaned the relays and replaced them. Then, using the screwdriver in her pocket, she adjusted the timer. "Keep your fingers crossed," she instructed.

The conveyor belt gave a strangled cough and began to move again. There was a moment's silence, then Raif exclaimed, "Nice work. Do you always keep a screwdriver in your shirt pocket?"

"When I'm driving Mehitabel I do. That's Sam's old pickup. It overheated about a mile back." Heather closed the control box as she added, "Sam and I have replaced nearly every nut and bolt in Mehitabel."

He looked enlightened. "I see. You and Sam are mechanics."

"I'm sort of an artist, actually. Sam used to own the Big S Garage before he passed away. My aunt Maggie is Sam's widow. It's because of her that I came to Mountain Farm."

She turned as she spoke, and the movement unsettled the bucket on which she'd been standing. As it lurched sideways, Heather tried to balance herself, but her hurt leg buckled. She would have fallen if Raif hadn't caught her by the arms and steadied her.

He frowned. "I'd feel better if you went to see the doctor about that leg. Please have the bill sent to me."

He sounded like a man used to getting his own way, and he had strong hands. As he helped her down, Heather had the sensation of being overwhelmed.

"That's not necessary," she murmured.

"It's the least I can do."

Somewhat to his surprise, Raif realized that he felt protective of Heather Leigh. Why, he had no idea, since she obviously could take care of herself. It was, he decided, because she'd helped him out even after being hurt by one of George's chickens. Also, he liked the scent that she wore. It seemed to be a distillation of sunshine and roses.

Heather was saying, "As I told you before, I've come here on Maggie's behalf."

She took a mental breath and slid into the pitch she had been practicing all the way to Mountain Farm. "Maggie's recently gone into the business of baking chiffon and meringue pies. You need eggs for that. Her pies are the best in the county and would cost ten dollars or more in a store. Yet she'd be willing to give you one of those pies for four dozen eggs."

"*Four* dozen eggs for one pie?" One dark eyebrow slanted up, and he looked unconvinced. Well, no one had said it would be easy. In the time-honored tradition of Mimosa, Heather settled herself to dicker.

"I forgive you for that look because, being an out-of-towner, you haven't tasted Maggie's pies. Her Key Lime Fluff is the talk of Mimosa, and then there's her Strawberry Rhubarb Cloud and her Mocha Almond Dream and her Lemon Meringue Mystery."

"A man could sell his soul for less."

And a man with a smile like that should be out-lawed, Heather thought. It was incredible how a movement of the lips could soften Raif's hard-planed face and make mischief dance in his eyes.

Aloud she said, "If you'll let me have four dozen eggs right now, I'll bring you a sample of Maggie's skills tomorrow. Do we have a deal?"

For a moment he hesitated, and she held her breath. Then he said, "In view of your, ah, services a few minutes ago, George should be grateful. I'm sure he'd be glad to give you a dozen eggs in return for scraping those relays."

"Considering the price of eggs these days, that's slave wages." Heather folded her arms across her breasts and rocked back on her heels. "If I hadn't reactivated the machinery, all of your friend's hens might have gone broody, and his production would have come to a halt. Besides, Maggie needs four dozen eggs."

He smiled that devastating smile of his and took a step closer to her. "That's asking a lot."

They were almost nose to nose. If she took a step forward, she could walk into his arms. Her instinct was to step back, but that would give him a psycho-logical advantage—or so she'd read in one of those assertiveness-training books.

He was continuing. "Instead of forty-eight eggs, what would you say to two of Maggie's pies for all the broken eggs collected each day?"

Heather narrowed her eyes. "Hold it right there. How many broken eggs are we talking about?"

"Figure it out for yourself. George keeps five thousand chickens. Each of them produces an average of one and a half eggs every two days." Raif looked wryly at the scattered feed on the ground. "He's supposed to have some local high school kids come by to sort and box them and clean up around here, too. So far, they haven't shown."

Five thousand chickens could lay a powerful lot of eggs, and from what she'd seen of the efficiency level of this farm so far, there'd surely be a lot of broken ones.

"It's a deal!" she cried.

As he returned Heather's smile, Raif ran a practiced eye over her trim figure. He approved of her piquant looks, her knockout legs and those capable little hands. And she wasn't bad when it came to negotiating a deal, either.

He was definitely going to enjoy getting to know this woman.

Chapter Two

By the time Heather returned with her water-filled milk containers, Mehitabel had cooled down. It was Heather's thermostat that was running high. She sang Sam's favorite ditty, "She'll Be Comin' Round the Mountain When She Comes," all the way back to Carver Street, and when she drew up to the old house with the tall pepper tree in back, she leaned on the horn.

Maggie came running down the back porch steps. Morning sunlight winked against her round, rimless glasses and on her neatly parted, tucked-back salt-and-pepper hair. "Well?" she demanded.

Heather banged her hand on Mehitabel's dented side. "Yes!"

"But how many pies do we have to give him for the eggs?"

"Maggie, this is a deal you can't refuse." Heather emerged from the pickup and struck a jaunty pose. "We're giving him two pies for all the brokens a day. With five thousand chickens laying, that could amount to a serious pile of eggs."

The smile that had been hovering around Maggie's lips burst forth. She looked as if she'd swallowed a sunrise. She hugged Heather, exclaiming, "You're a caution, Heather Leigh. I always told Sam you were the best bargainer in the family."

She had spoken Sam's name without sorrow or pain, and Heather felt a surge of relief. She'd been worried about Maggie ever since she and her then-fiancé Bill Reese had flown down from New York to attend Sam's funeral last May. Though the older woman had tried to sound cheerful during their weekly phone calls, the emptiness in her voice had scared Heather.

Many times Heather had wanted to fly back to Mimosa and check on Maggie personally, but she'd still been engaged to Bill then, and she'd also been on his team of designers. They'd been working on getting ready a TV commercial, and Bill had made it quite plain that if she left New York now she'd not only be abandoning her work but deserting him personally.

Three months later, she and Bill had broken it off. Heather had hoped to return to Mimosa over Thanksgiving break but instead had worked through the weekend. Since Bill had been promoted to vice president in charge of design, the workload had tripled. She'd felt exhausted all the time and depressed most of the time, and the work she'd once enjoyed had begun to stifle her.

Christmas had found her down with the flu and then, on New Year's Day, Maggie had phoned. As she'd told Heather about her desire to go into the pie-making business, she'd sounded anxious, unsure and yet more eager and alive than she'd sounded in a long while. "I've always loved baking, and folks have liked my pies. I feel I could make a go of it." She paused. "What do you think, sugar? I feel that Sam would want me to go ahead, but maybe that's wishful thinking."

Heather suddenly had a mental image of that big, sweet guy beaming with approval. "I think it's a wonderful idea," she cried. "I only wish I could be there to help—"

And then she'd stopped short in midsentence and asked herself, why not? What's to stop me?

She'd made plans in a hurry, quit her job with a feeling very much like relief, and sublet her uptown efficiency. She'd stored her possessions with friends and booked a flight to Tampa. As an excuse for her return, she'd told Maggie that she needed a change from Pattersons and Lowell. "I need to touch base again," she'd said.

And it was true. It was good to be back in Mimosa, back with home folks, and above all good to be with Maggie. In Maggie's company, Heather could forget the ache that she'd felt ever since she and Bill had parted company.

The first night they'd been together, they'd talked until the wee hours. Maggie, naturally, had wanted to talk about Bill Reese and why the engagement had gone sour, but Heather had kept steering her back to the subject of her pies. Heather had assured her that she would handle all the promotion and advertising, then they'd spent some time thinking of a catchy name for Maggie's venture. It didn't come till Kenny Styles, the postman, stopped the next day with a package Heather had mailed herself from New York, and stayed for coffee and one of Maggie's pies. "No wonder I gain weight," he'd complained. "This Key Lime Fluff is mmm-delicious."

"That's it—MM Pies," Heather had cried. "Get it? MM for Maggie Munroe."

Now, bringing home good news, she felt equally triumphant. "We can scratch eggs off your list of expenses," she said. "Tomorrow I pick up our first batch of free eggs."

Maggie was frowning. "There's blood on your pants leg."

"I'll tell you about it over a cup of coffee." But in fact, the story was told as she helped the older woman assemble ingredients for one of Maggie's meringue pies. Maggie was by turns horrified, amused and thoughtful.

"Raif Cornell. Seems like the name rings a bell." She considered it several moments, then shook her head. "Ah, well, my memory's shot."

They got to work and the afternoon flowed smoothly by. Used to the hectic pace of working in a New York advertising agency, Heather had to shift gears, adjust her internal clock to Mimosa's lack of speed.

They were clearing up when Heather heard the sound of wheels. Maggie pushed her glasses back on her nose, exclaiming, "I told Avery to come by for dinner, but it's an hour too early. What's he thinking about?"

But instead of the accountant's dingy blue car, a serviceable black pickup pulled into the driveway. Heather stared in astonishment as Raif Cornell emerged. "What's he doing here?" she wondered.

Maggie's brow puckered. "Oh, I'll bet he's had second thoughts about those eggs."

Followed closely by Maggie, Heather headed toward the front porch. "Can I help you?" she called.

Raif glanced at the formidable-looking lady who was standing behind Heather, and explained, "I thought you might need a few eggs."

He held out a stack of paper cartons and Heather exclaimed, "Good grief, are all those eggs broken?"

"The kids George hired finally showed up to do their picking and cleaning routine. They'd just been to a basketball game, and I think they hit a lot of high fives while handling the eggs."

The older woman grinned, and Raif registered surprise that she could pack such a dynamite smile.

"I can't tell you how glad I am to see you, Raif," she cried, then introduced herself. "Come in, come in. And bring those gorgeous eggs with you."

Heather held open the screen door for him. As he passed her, his bare arm brushed hers. It was a hard arm, muscled like the rest of him, and Heather wondered what Raif Cornell did for a living. He'd mentioned a Boston-based firm, and he'd been to Boston

University. Perhaps he was a business major like his friend George, but she doubted it. No pencil pusher could have that broad-shouldered, lean-waisted build.

Did he lift weights in his spare time? But Raif didn't have one of those square, no-neck physiques she'd so often seen emerging from the gym near her New York apartment. Still speculating, Heather followed Raif and Maggie into the house.

"I'm putting up a pot of coffee," Maggie announced. "Sugar, show Raif where the spare fridge is."

The ancient refrigerator was in a pantry just off the old-fashioned kitchen. It was a small room with shelves lined with sparkling jars of jellies, preserves and pickles. An ancient upright freezer stood beside the fridge.

"Maggie has a garden," Heather explained. She opened the freezer so Raif could see the rows of neatly packaged vegetables. "She freezes enough for an army."

Somewhat to her surprise, he lifted out a package of corn and examined it carefully before nodding his approval. "Nicely done," he commented, "but I don't see any of those famous pies. Don't they freeze well?"

He replaced the vegetables as he spoke, and his hand brushed hers. The casual contact affected her like a spurt of electricity. Instinctively Heather moved backward and found herself pressed against his lean length.

She hadn't realized before just how small the pantry was. There was barely room for two people—scarcely room to breathe, in fact. That would explain her sudden sense of light-headedness and the fact that she was acutely aware of the cologne Raif wore. It wasn't casual or obvious but something both subtle and vibrant and most definitely male.

Heather frowned a little. What had they been talking about? Ah, yes. Pies.

"They do freeze well, but Maggie prefers to make them fresh. In fact, she's been baking all day for her customers. Want to see?"

She managed to slide by him into the kitchen where a dozen pies cooled on the counter. Raif hardly glanced at them, however. "Do you have a moment?" he asked. "I need to pick your brains." She nodded and he added, "I was wondering if you knew someone who painted signs."

Heather recalled the dilapidated sign she had missed so often this morning. "You mean for Mountain Farm?"

"Yes. I'd like to give George something useful as a thank-you gift before I leave. I looked in the phone book, but the nearest sign painter is someplace in Clearwater."

"Maybe Maggie would know." Heather paused. "Or I could handle it."

Just then Maggie interrupted. "Sugar, where are your manners? Standing around there chatting when the man drove all the way out here to bring us those eggs. Offer Raif a cup of coffee and take him to set out under the pepper tree for a spell. I'd invite you all to visit in the kitchen with me, but it's mighty messy right now."

Heather complied, and Raif watched her pouring coffee from a battered old percolator into a mug that said I Love New York. He liked the way she moved, and the coffee she handed him was delicious. It had a rich, nutty flavor and tasted light years better than the instant variety they drank at George's farm.

As they left the kitchen and went down the back porch stairs, Raif watched her. He liked the way she walked with a spring to her step that somehow managed to be completely feminine. She'd changed into cream-colored chinos and an oversize blue sweatshirt that had Big S stenciled across the front. It certainly wasn't Newbury Street or Fifth Avenue, but on Heather the combination looked good, Raif thought appreciatively as he followed her to a slatted wooden bench that had been positioned under the spreading branches of a pepper tree.

Lying on the bench was a drawing pad. He picked it up. "Yours?"

"Just some sketches for flyers advertising Maggie's new venture. I must have left them out here."

She was offhanded, but Raif was astonished. When she'd said she was an artist, he'd figured she made a few dollars selling Florida landscapes to tourists. He hadn't expected the sophistication and skill that flowed out of these sketches.

"You should be in advertising," he exclaimed.

She didn't actually sigh, but a shadow seemed to touch her eyes. "I used to work for Pattersons and Lowell, a New York agency."

As she spoke, he leaned back against the rough wooden slats and watched her. It was a trick he'd learned at the bargaining table, a ploy that enabled him to learn far more than what was being said. But whereas the people he usually dealt with had much to hide, Heather's extraordinary hazel eyes reflected all her emotions. You could look into them and see exactly what she was thinking.

Heather Leigh was an original, and interesting to a degree that Raif found surprising. Though hardly a playboy, he'd never lacked female companionship. Until a few months ago, in fact, there had been a steady lady in his life—Monica Hardy, who'd been everything he wanted in a woman. But Monica, beautiful, glamorous and smart daughter to Senator Paul Hardy, had ambitions. She wanted her husband to be a political figure.

That wasn't for Raif, and their romantic involvement had ended by mutual consent. They'd remained friends. Would an affair with Heather Leigh have as civilized an ending? he wondered, and felt a surge of interest. An affair with Heather—now that was an intriguing idea.

Under that oversize sweatshirt, Raif sensed that Heather would be sleek and slender but rounded in all the right places. He also had the notion that she'd fit comfortably into his arms.

It took some effort to call back his wandering thoughts and listen to what she was saying. "I worked for P. and L. for three years." Heather absently rubbed flour off the knee of her chinos. "Now that I'm back in Mimosa, I can use what I learned to help Maggie."

"From looking at those sketches, I'd say you'll be a real help." There was true approval in Raif's voice and more in his eyes, and he reached for her hand as he spoke. The clasp of his big hand over hers sent shivers up her arm. *Warm* shivers.

Casually withdrawing her hand, Heather said, "I'm glad you came over, so that you can sample one of Maggie's pies. I'm sure you never ate anything like them in Boston."

As if on cue, the older woman appeared on the back porch steps. "Aren't you two cold sitting out there? It's warm for during the day, but it cools down fast when the sun goes down."

Vaguely, Heather looked toward the west. The sun had indeed gone down, leaving dull russet and violet streamers in its wake.

Maggie continued, "I was going to offer you a slice of my Key Lime Fluff, Raif, but I've got a better idea. Why not stay for dinner? My accountant, Avery Lewis, will be over, too."

Heather observed Raif's look of surprise and guessed that this wasn't the way things were done in Boston. To give him a way to back out gracefully she said, "You and your friend probably have other plans."

Mentally, Raif reviewed the three six-packs of beer and the stone-hard pizza that George's refrigerator contained. "No plans. But I don't want to put you out, Mrs. Munroe."

"Raif, Mrs. Munroe is Sam's grandmother. Call me by my name." Maggie looked back over her shoulder to add, "Maybe we'd best use the dining room since we've got company, Heather."

Raif immediately denied that he was company and said that dining rooms make him nervous. "That's what my Sam used to say," Maggie said approvingly.

She shot a speculative look at the tall man as he walked into the kitchen. "You married, Raif?" When he shook his head, she clicked her tongue. "I don't know about girls these days. A likely fellow like you should have been snapped up long ago."

Heather scowled at Maggie, but the warning was ignored. "Maybe there's someone special back home?" Maggie purred.

"When is Avery expected?" Heather interrupted almost desperately, but nothing was going to deflect Maggie from her matchmaking.

"Nobody special right now, Maggie," Raif was saying. He shot Heather an amused look and added, "But I'm open to suggestion."

Heather was disgusted with the warmth in her cheeks. She glared at Maggie, who said innocently, "Sugar, you want to climb on a chair and get the good plates from the top shelf?"

"Can I help?" While Heather was dragging the step stool over, Raif came up behind her. He reached the top shelf easily, and their hands met amongst the plates.

Love amongst the crockery. Oh, for God's sake, Heather, be real!

The way things were going, Heather was grateful when Avery's car clanked up to the house. She kept on being grateful, even though skinny, pinch-mouthed

Avery was hardly her favorite person. He might be a crackerjack accountant, but almost every word out of his mouth was a criticism, and his idea of scintillating conversation was a monologue about how Mimosa was changing for the worse.

"We're a small community," Avery lectured. "That's how we like it here, and that's how it should stay. Used to be, I knew everybody in town. Now you find strangers everywhere, and they all drive like crazy. No wonder they put up a traffic light at Four Corners." He shook his head over this sign of decadence and added, "Then there's that new Cozee Motel they're building up to Route 19, and I heard talk just today that a new condo complex is going up near Brooksville. That's going to mean even more traffic."

Maggie said warningly, "You'll make Raif think we're hicks, Avery. Mimosa must be the boondocks after Boston."

"I think Mimosa is pretty wonderful," Raif replied. "The fishing is terrific, and it's so quiet at Mountain Farm I can hear myself think. You've got a beautiful town here."

Was he being sarcastic? But he looked totally sincere. He'd been tucking into Maggie's pot roast and homemade bread, and now he looked relaxed and content. When he caught Heather's eye, he smiled at her. "Really beautiful."

Now, was that a compliment or was she reaching? But she didn't have time to follow that thought because Maggie was exclaiming, "Mimosa can't stay in the dark ages forever, Avery. Besides, more people mean more customers for my pies."

Avery was a small man with a narrow face, and his frown seemed to take up most of his forehead. "I'm not sure that your pies are such a good idea, Maggie," he said. "I don't know what Sam would say if he knew you were using your savings to back perishables. Pies spoil quickly, and then where are your profits?"

Seeing the flicker of doubt in Maggie's eyes, Heather came to the rescue. "Maggie's pies are too good to spoil, Avery. I guarantee there won't be a crumb left of our dessert." She smiled at the older woman, asking, "Shall I go get the pièce de résistance?"

"No, I will." Maggie rose from the table. "You clear up, sugar, and I'll serve up the pie."

The pie surpassed all of Raif's expectations. It was a magnificent concoction that stood almost a foot high, and it tasted even better than it looked. The meringue was marvelously textured, and the lime-flavored cream cheese went down like silk. Raif saw the questioning look in Heather's eyes and kissed his fingers in an exaggerated gesture. "My compliments to the chef. This is the best pie I've ever eaten."

Maggie beamed. Heather relaxed, then frowned again as Avery pointed out, "Good to eat, I grant you. But everyone in Mimosa makes pies."

"Not like these. I'm in the food business back in Boston," Raif added, "and these pies are truly superb."

"What's the name of your food business?" When told, Avery pursed his lips. "Raifoods, eh? Seems to me I heard of it someplace. But if you're in the business, Cornell, you'll be the first to say that small businesses stand to fail in this day and age."

It was all Heather could do to restrain herself from kicking Avery. She glared at him and stated, "MM Pies won't fail."

Avery only shrugged gloomily, but Raif asked, "How do you plan to market the pies?"

Heather took charge. "We've printed flyers and have distributed them to area businesses. Maggie's friends and I plan to hand them out at local shopping malls. We've also given out some free pies so we can get endorsements of our product." Encouraged by Raif's nod, she added, "We've put an ad in the *Mimosa Herald* and in the weekly shopper's guide that gets mailed out to all the homes in the area."

"Have you done an analysis of your competition?" Raif asked.

"Maggie *has* no competition. Her pies are tops."

Raif smiled at Heather's firm tone. "I'm sure they are, but not everyone knows that. Do you plan to profile the prospects you want to reach? Clients are what it's all about, as you know yourself."

"Let me show you." Heather left the table but soon returned with a notebook. She went to Raif and spread the notebook open as she added, "I've made a list of all the old and new businesses in the area, then broken it down to those firms that would be most interested in Maggie's product. We're going to mail these people a letter offering them a one-time deal if they place orders now."

What she was saying made sense, but Raif was much more aware of her physical nearness. Her perfume teased him, and when he moved his head to look up at her, her curls brushed his cheek. It took some effort to say, "So you've already analyzed your market."

Heather nodded eagerly, but Avery snorted. "She's talked to a few locals. That's not a market analysis."

"Now hold on just a minute," Maggie exploded. "Jim Henderson at the Mimosa Hotel isn't any local yokel. And so isn't Norma Lighten, and Andy Barre, who just happens to be a caterer, and there are lots more I could name. Every living one of them loved my pies. They'll give me orders."

Raif's eyes swept Maggie's homey but old-fashioned kitchen. "How many pies could you turn out in a day, Maggie?" She told him. "That would be enough to start with. Eventually you'll need a more modern oven, as well as workers to help you."

"I don't know as that would be necessary," Maggie protested.

"You've got to be prepared for your pies becoming big sellers, Maggie. You're at the right place at the right time. West central Florida is growing fast as Avery pointed out, and that means more restaurants, specialized bakeries, hotels and so forth. And since Heather says that the pies freeze well, they can eventually be shipped out of state."

"Out of *state*?"

Maggie almost breathed the question, and her eyes held an awed look. "Maybe we'd better start by concentrating on orders we can get in Mimosa," Heather said.

Heedless of Avery's continued grumbling, they spent the rest of the evening discussing MM Pies. Heather blessed Raif for his enthusiasm and also for his excellent ideas. She'd thought she knew a lot about advertising strategy, but Raif definitely had the edge on her.

Even Avery was impressed. "You seem to know what you're doing," he allowed as Raif got up to leave. "I'd like to ask you some more questions, but you probably have to get up with the chickens." Maggie looked pained and Heather rolled her eyes, but Avery was so pleased with his joke that he cackled with laughter.

Raif started to shake Maggie's hand, then kissed her cheek instead. The older woman beamed as he added, "Thank you for the best meal I've had in months."

"And thank *you*," Heather said as she walked out with him into the chilly night. "Maggie needs a lot of encouragement."

"I can believe it. Starting something new can be as frightening as it's exciting."

He half turned to look at her, and something caught in Heather's heart. Starting something new—was that what they were doing?

She gave herself a vigorous mental shake. It was Maggie they were discussing, for heaven's sake. "Did you mean it when you said her pies could eventually be marketed out of state?"

The golden half-moon in the sky lined his bold profile as he nodded. "If they're all as special as the one I had tonight, she won't be able to bake them fast enough. Of course there's the problem of how to retain quality while producing quantity."

He'd spoken automatically, for business was the furthest thing from his mind just now. He was too busy admiring the way the moon dusted gold onto Heather's curls and drew delectable shadows about her mouth.

Why was he looking at her so intently? And why, Heather asked herself, was she feeling both cold and hot at the same time? It was almost as though Maggie's dandelion wine, which they'd all sipped after dinner, had gone to her head.

"Maggie has worked hard all her life," she said, "but never outside the home. Sam was a good provider as well as being a great human being."

"You loved him very much," he said.

"My parents were killed in an accident when I was ten, you see, and I came to live with Sam and Maggie. They were always there for me."

As they began to move forward again, their shoulders bumped gently. Raif felt Heather shiver and almost unthinkingly put his arm around her. "Is that better?" he murmured.

Now how was she supposed to respond to that? Unable to explain the soft electric shocks that were imploding under her skin, Heather stepped hastily out of his encircling arm. Immediately, she started shivering again.

"You'd better go back inside before you freeze," Raif suggested.

But he was lying through his teeth. He didn't want Heather to go into the house. What he *really* wanted—

Raif gave his lustful mind a slap and dragged it back to reality.

"We got sidetracked this afternoon. If you remember, you said you could handle a sign for Mountain Farm."

In the darkness, Raif could see her delicate eyebrows draw together into a pucker of concentration. "How fast do you want it done?"

"As soon as possible. I'd like to give it to George before I leave for Boston."

Catching the changed note in his voice, Heather knew that in spite of his obvious liking for Mimosa, Raif wanted to get home to the East Coast. She brushed a tug of regret aside to say, "I'll get to it as soon as I finish the work I'm doing for Maggie."

His eyes smiled down into hers. "That's good enough for me. What's the going rate for signs in Mimosa? Or would you prefer more eggs?"

"M-more eggs, I think."

Heather was surprised at herself for stammering like this. But, she rationalized, it was because the night was turning colder by the minute. Her goose bumps had goose bumps, for heaven's sake.

She tried for a no-nonsense tone. "It looks as if we've made another bargain."

"Absolutely."

She caught her breath at the vibrant note in his voice, the look in his eyes. "I think I'd better get back," Heather began.

Instead of responding, he rested his hands on her shoulders. For a long moment they searched each other's faces. He leaned forward. So did she. It seemed as though the night itself was holding its breath. Then, unhurriedly, Raif lowered his mouth to hers.

Chapter Three

His lips were cool, but they generated heat. Somewhere inside Heather, a chain reaction of soft explosions had begun. They drifted like dandelion-down through her body until each separate artery and vein was tingling with aftershock.

This was a kiss, but even this thought disappeared as Raif's tongue traced the curve of her mouth, teasing her until she felt positively weak-kneed.

Automatically clinging to Raif for support, she was very aware of the rasp of his cheek against hers, the warmth and strength of his arms as they closed around her. It was, Heather thought, as though she'd been wrapped in sheet lightning.

An unbidden thought reminded her Bill's kisses had never made her feel this way. At the moment Heather could hardly remember Bill's face, and she definitely didn't want to think of him, but trying not to think shattered the mood. Suddenly and jarringly aware of what was happening, Heather pushed herself away from the hard body she'd been leaning on.

Raif didn't want to let her go. Just as he'd imagined, Heather's slender curves had nestled perfectly into his arms. But as he reluctantly loosened those arms from around her, he saw that she looked wary. He wondered why. She'd enjoyed the kiss as much as he had—or at least, it had seemed that way.

"It's getting downright cold," Heather was saying. It wasn't easy to act casual when every cell in her body seemed to be awake and quivering, but she managed to add, "Good night," and walk a relatively straight line back toward Maggie's front porch.

Saying good-night was the last thing that Raif wanted to do, but he reminded himself he'd only met the woman today and that this wasn't New York or Boston but the backwaters of Florida. Apparently, everything here progressed slowly.

He said, "I'll see you soon, Heather," and his deep voice made a caress of her name. Immediately, the dandelion-fluff madness began circulating through her veins again, and Heather couldn't help hesitating.

Raif saw her pause and tried to think of a delaying tactic that would keep her with him. His normally fertile mind drew a blank, and all he could think of to say was, "I really hope you get a chance to do that sign for George before I leave."

The swift transition to business made Heather blink. "When *do* you leave?"

"Sunday," he replied and felt genuine regret that he had only six more days in Mimosa. But he'd been gone for nearly a week, and though Danny Hoaas, his able vice president in charge of marketing, and Ted Kovacheck could manage things well in his absence, he was anxious to get back into the action.

Heather noted that Raif's eyes now held a faraway expression. "I'll do my best," she said.

"Good night, then," he said. He was smiling at her again, but somehow the smile didn't affect Heather as it had done before.

Raif's preoccupied look was oddly familiar. She'd seen its twin on Bill's face a thousand times. And she could bet her boots that that million-miles-away expression meant Raif was absorbed in matters that had nothing to do with Heather Leigh.

Heather bought the wood for George's sign next day. She'd meant to tell Raif about it when she went to collect eggs for Maggie, but he wasn't around. It was George himself who handed her three large cartons of slightly damaged eggs.

"Raiford told me what you did for me," George boomed in his basso profundo. "I'm grateful, ma'am."

In a few minutes, they'd gone beyond the "ma'am" and "Mr. Montfort" stage, and were chatting like old friends. It was refreshing, Heather noted, to realize that here was a man with no hidden crevices or corners to his character. What you saw was what you got—a six-foot-plus giant with an ingenuous smile.

When George learned that she'd been in advertising, he got a gleam in his eye and asked if Heather could do up some creative newspaper ads for him.

"My farm needs a helping hand," he explained. "In fact, it could do with a whole bunch of hands." A sigh rippled through his bulky torso as he added, "It's my fault. I broke every rule in the book. I bought Mountain Farm on impulse. I didn't have enough cash flow to support me for more than a couple of months. I thought eggs would be an easy way to make money and that I could learn the trade as I went along."

"Perhaps your friend could help," Heather pointed out. "He seems to know a great deal about the food business."

"He knows pretty nearly everything about the food business, and he'd help me in a minute if I let him, but Raiford is on a much-needed vacation." George paused to add hopefully, "Do you think you could work on those ads for me, Heather?"

She said she'd do so and on her way home revolved some ideas in her mind. But there was no time to work on sketches that day. When Heather returned home with her eggs, she found Maggie determinedly beating eggs and talking on the phone.

"That Avery Lewis," Maggie moaned. "He's really done it this time."

"What? What's he done? If he's been talking down MM Pies, I'll go and punch him out," Heather vowed.

But Maggie shook her head. "He hasn't been talking us down. He's just been talking. Sugar, he's told everyone that I'm going into the pie-making business, and everybody and her cousin has been phoning and ordering." As if on cue the phone began to shrill again. "Oh, gosh durn it, anyway. I'm going to have a nervous breakdown."

There was a huge blob of meringue on Maggie's nose, a dab of flour on her gaunt cheek, and her eyes looked definitely wild. In spite of this, Maggie appeared happier than she'd done since Sam's death.

Between several more phone calls, Heather helped Maggie put pies together. They made a dozen pies that afternoon, and Heather delivered them while Maggie soldiered on in the kitchen. The phone kept ringing until Maggie took it off the hook.

"And to think I came back to Mimosa to rest," Heather couldn't help teasing as they put up the final batch of pies for the day.

Maggie gave her a keen look. "Sure you didn't come home for another reason? I'd have thought it was because you broke up with Bill Reese."

When Maggie had something on her mind, she could get downright blunt. Heather knew that it was no use to try to avoid the subject any longer, so she said, "We just didn't see things the same way."

Would Maggie leave it now? No, she would not. "Sugar, everyone's made different," she lectured. "You didn't let that handsome young man get away just because you two had a disagreement?"

Repressing a sigh, Heather said, "Bill loved his work."

"So what? Lots of women I know would give their eyeteeth for a man who worked."

"I mean that Bill loved his work too much. He was a workaholic." Heather could see Maggie's lips moving silently on the word as she continued, "Workaholics love their work more than anything or anyone on earth. Bill would get involved in some project of his and forget what time it was, forget to eat, forget he had appointments or dates or whatever."

"You mean he stood you up?" Maggie wanted to know.

"Sure he did. Sometimes he'd phone at the last minute, but more often than not he'd just forget, like the time he was supposed to pick me up at the airport. Another time, he left me standing at the theater with tickets I'd bought him for his birthday."

Heather didn't tell Maggie that she'd got up at four o'clock on an icy February morning and stood in line for five hours in order to get those tickets. She hadn't even been particularly crazy about the rock-and-roll group, but they were Bill's favorite. When he didn't show at the theater, she'd been frantic with worry that he'd gotten into an accident.

"He didn't make the concert, but that didn't matter. You see," Heather broke off to explain, "I made excuses for him all the time. Advertising is a high-powered, competitive field, and Bill was a talented and ambitious man. But things just went from bad to worse."

Maggie looked mournful. "And I thought he was such a nice man when he came down for Sam's funeral. I thought you looked so happy together."

"Bill *was* nice." Heather fluted a piecrust as she added, "He loved me, but he loved the idea of becoming vice president in charge of design even more. When he was after something, nothing else existed for him or mattered to him."

Not even me. Though Heather hadn't said the words, they seemed to shadow the warm, fragrant kitchen until she said crisply, "Well, it's water under the bridge now."

Maggie rubbed her nose with a floury hand. "Sugar, I'm glad you came home even if you only did it 'cause you were worried about me."

Ignoring the lump in her throat, Heather hugged the older woman. "That's all you know. I just got home-sick for your Key Lime Fluff."

They went to bed late and rose early to the shrilling phone. Heather did manage to do rough sketches for George's ad and drop them off at Mountain Farm when she collected the day's broken eggs. Other than this, she was kept busy baking and delivering pies.

"You're probably going to need a staff of bakers," Heather pointed out to Maggie the next day.

"I can't afford to do that just yet, but I've been thinking on it ever since Raif said those exact words to me." Maggie paused. "How is he, by the way?"

Heather was careful to keep her voice neutral. "I haven't seen him since he came here."

"Too bad he's going back to Boston so soon. Let's invite him to dinner before he leaves, huh? That'd be a nice, friendly thing to do."

Maggie's innocent tone didn't fool Heather for a moment. "George says he's been fishing and sunning from sunup to sundown."

"Now, I'd say that was what you needed," Maggie exclaimed. "You've been working too hard, sugar. You need to loosen up."

Perhaps, Heather thought, she could take an hour or so of R and R before going up to Mountain Farm for more eggs. "I might drive out to Pine Lagoon," she told Maggie, who immediately said she'd pack a little lunch.

Heather went up to her room, changed into shorts and a tank top and pulled out an old bikini she hadn't worn in years. Then, on impulse, she pulled out her old sketchbook and pastels. Somehow Pine Lagoon and her sketchbook seemed to go together.

It was a magnificent day, warm and windless. Sunlight and bird song and the familiar trail brought memories. How many times, Heather wondered, had she and Sam taken a lunch and driven out to the secluded spot together? They'd said little to each other as he fished and she sketched, but she'd never felt so at peace and happy. She hoped that the place hadn't changed.

It hadn't. The dirt road that led to the lagoon was still nearly impassable, and Mehitabel lurched along, clanking and complaining, past a forest of scrub pines and palmetto. At her approach egrets fled screeching, and a regal blue heron looked down disapprovingly from an oak branch festooned with Spanish moss. Heather drew a deep breath of pine-scented air and felt the lagoon welcome her home.

Soon the road narrowed to a footpath. Heather pulled Mehitabel into the shadow of some pepper trees and, picking up her sketchbook and the basket with her sandwiches and bikini, walked the last half mile to the lagoon. For a while the trees shaded her, but soon they gave way to a clearing full of sunshine. Then she was staring at incredibly blue water.

Pine Lagoon wasn't very large, but today it seemed to stretch forever before disappearing into the afternoon haze. Herons fished in the tree-shadowed shallows while pelicans, looking like miniature pterodactyls in flight, dived for fish. Happily, Heather sank down on a grass bank and began to sketch.

"Hey, you're really good."

Startled, Heather looked up and saw Raif leaning over her shoulder. "When d-did you get here?" she stammered.

"A few minutes ago."

She'd been so absorbed in her sketching she hadn't heard him, let alone seen him come down the path. So much for the survival instincts she'd picked up in New York. A mugger could have stomped right up to her before she realized which planet she was on.

Heather looked more carefully at Raif and saw that he was wearing his cutoffs and a muscle T-shirt that had a football helmet on it and the logo, Go, Bucaneers. He was also carrying a six-pack.

"Where's the fishing rod?" she asked.

"I wasn't going fishing. I've been looking for you. I've been trying to phone you, but your phone rang busy, so I finally drove down to Maggie's. She told me you'd be out here, and I figured that by now you'd have worked up a thirst."

Raif shook his six-pack invitingly. The warmth in his smile was another invitation. Trying to ignore the fact that her temperature had nudged up several degrees, Heather said, "I'm sorry I haven't got to George's sign yet."

"That's okay. Actually, I just wanted to see you again."

His green eyes shimmered with contagious pleasure. As he sat down next to her on the grass, sunlight
caught the blue highlights in his dark hair. He was so
close to her that if she moved a muscle, they'd touch.
Even the air was invaded by his subtle after-shave and
the clean, outdoors scent of the man himself.

"I like the way you've caught the sunlight on the
water," Raif commented. He'd leaned closer to her,
and Heather could feel his warm breath on her cheek.
When his arm brushed hers, the hairs on her arms felt
static with electricity.

Determined to put some distance between herself
and Raif, she scooted her bottom a few inches away.
Promptly, as though it were the most natural thing in
the world, he followed her lead so that one strong-
muscled thigh pressed lightly against hers.

This was going from bad to worse. In an attempt to
regroup and retrench, Heather said, "I dropped some
roughs off for George's ad yesterday. Did you see
them?"

"They're very good. Let's hope a creative ad gen-
erates business for him."

Raif sounded troubled, and Heather remembered
what George had said about Raif's wanting to help.
"Is Mountain Farm in deep trouble?" she asked.

"Chicken farms usually make their profit by con-
tracting their eggs exclusively to large concerns.
George tried that route, but he was underbid." Absently, Raif reached out a hand and brushed back a
curl that had fallen across Heather's forehead.

His lightest touch seemed to do weird things to her
pulse. This had to stop, and now. Heather got to her

feet, muttering, "I need a different angle if I'm going to get the effect I want."

"Seems to me the effect is terrific the way it is."

And for sure he meant it. With the sun turning her curls into a golden halo, Heather was a picture worth looking at. Raif leaned back on an elbow and watched appreciatively as Heather sat down on a felled tree some distance away and began to sketch again. He liked the way her hands moved, the little pucker between her delicate brows. In fact, he liked everything about Heather. Unfortunately, he was set to return to Boston in a few days.

"It's too bad." He hadn't realized he was thinking aloud until she looked up at him.

"You mean about George?" she asked.

Not wanting to admit that George had been the furthest thing from his mind, Raif said gravely, "He wouldn't thank us for discussing his problems. Are you getting thirsty yet?"

"Sure am. And hungry, too." Heather put down her sketch pad and opened the lunch basket. As usual, Maggie had packed enough tuna fish, egg and tomato sandwiches to satisfy a dozen ravenous linebackers.

"I'll barter one of these sandwiches for a beer," Heather suggested.

"Good deal." Raif popped one of the cans and handed it to her. Their hands touched, and Heather was aware of the contrast between the icy-cold can and Raif's warm, strong fingers. "Let's drink to MM Pies."

"To MM Pies," she agreed.

Raif decided he liked the way Heather drank beer, too. He watched the swallow shapes her delicate throat made, and the way her pink tongue licked the foam from her generous, pink mouth brought back memories of their kiss.

"Why are you smiling?" Heather wanted to know.

"Was I?"

"Grinning, actually. You look like a cat that's swallowed a whole team of canaries." But Heather was smiling, too. It was a lighthearted kind of day, lazy and rich with sunshine and deep, blue sky. Suddenly, she felt ridiculously happy. "Isn't this the life?"

"Tuna fish sandwiches, beer and thou," Raif quipped, but he knew he hadn't felt so good in a long time. He finished his sandwich and offered her another beer. "Same terms?"

"No beer for me, but have another sandwich and try these cookies." Raif's eyes widened as Heather unwrapped half a dozen enormous chocolate chip cookies. "When Maggie packs a lunch, she packs a lunch. Many times Sam and I could hardly carry the basket between us."

Her voice had softened to a reminiscent note and Raif gazed out over the shimmering water. This was truly a place for memories, he thought. Pine Lagoon reminded him of the times he and his dad had gone out fishing off Falmouth. Those had been days of struggle for Raifoods but somehow they'd found the time for a few hours together.

Dad, I wish you could know we've turned out okay. As the thought touched Raif's mind, Heather said,

"Your stay in Mimosa is nearly over. Are you missing Boston?"

"I worry about how things are going at Raifoods," he admitted. "There are some loose ends in a recent acquisition that need to be tied up."

For a moment his thoughts seemed to drift away. Then he refocused. Flipping over on his side, he smiled up at her. "But this isn't the kind of day to talk business. Let's talk about you."

Leaning over, he rubbed a finger lightly across Heather's arm. "Why did you really come back to the old hometown?"

His deep voice had softened to a confiding purr. If she wasn't careful, Heather knew, she'd end up telling this man every secret she'd ever had. Carefully she said, "Besides Maggie needing me, you mean? I felt that I needed a change from the excitement and the craziness. I guess that means I'm just a country mouse at heart."

There was a guarded note in her voice and shadows in her candid hazel eyes. Raif knew she wasn't telling him everything, that she was thinking of some sorrow that had nothing to do with Sam's death. Suddenly he wanted to put his arms around Heather and hold her close to him. He wanted to kiss her and take the shadows away.

There was a splash nearby as a huge brown pelican dived down from the sky. A moment later it emerged, lower beak bulging and spilling water. "Where else can you eat and swim for the same price?" Heather chuckled.

Raif looked interested. "Is the water safe for swimming? I mean, do alligators and snakes hang out in there?"

She shook her head. "They live in fresh water. Saltwater swimming is safe here in Florida."

"In that case what are we waiting for? Let's peel out of our clothes and dive in."

She turned to look full at him and saw that he was grinning tantalizingly at her. "Didn't you bring your bathing suit?" she asked sternly.

"Did you?"

"Of course I did." Heather was pleased to see him look momentarily disconcerted, and added severely, "Were you suggesting that we go skinny-dipping? If you were, I'll have you know that there's a fine. Since nobody wants to pay fifty dollars a dip, Mimosans carry a suit when they come to Pine Lagoon."

He muttered something that sounded vaguely like, "It'd be worth it." Aloud he said, "I suppose I could swim in my cutoffs. Is there a cabana someplace where you can change?"

She waved her arm toward a clump of palmetto palms. "You're looking at it."

"Unisex, huh?"

She tried to frown, but laughter brimmed in her eyes as she got to her feet. "Watch your step, mister. None of your city-slicker tricks in Mimosa."

His laughter followed Heather as she walked toward the swaying palms. Although she was sure that the thick growth completely screened her from view, she undressed quickly. She was very conscious of

Raif's presence and her bare skin tingled with nerves until she'd pulled on her bikini.

Then she gazed down at herself in dismay. Either she'd gained a few pounds or the bikini had shrunk and the once-bright colors had faded. Heather sighed in resignation. She'd come here to swim, after all, not to put on a fashion show.

Raif was already waist-deep in water when she emerged from the palms, and his appreciative whistle was echoed by the look in his eyes. Pretending an indifference she was far from feeling, Heather walked briskly up to the lagoon.

"Come on in," Raif invited. "The water's fine."

Heather entered the lagoon slowly, letting her warm body grow accustomed by degrees to the cool of the water. She couldn't help noticing how sunlight glinted on Raif's broad shoulders and gilded the dark hair that covered his broad chest and lean waist until it dipped down under the waistband of his cutoffs.

"What's taking you so long?" he called.

His voice snapped the spell that had held her. But as Heather took a step forward, something slimy slid underfoot. With a startled yelp, Heather hopped into the air, lost her footing and disappeared under the water.

She emerged a few seconds later, sputtering and coughing. "The creature from the Pine Lagoon attacked you?" Raif wanted to know.

"Very funny." Heather dashed water from her eyes and scowled, which apparently encouraged Raif to laugh harder.

"You gave a little gurgle and then you sank out of sight. Is that some Mimosan water ritual, because if so—"

He broke off as Heather let out a bloodcurdling shriek. "Alligator to one o'clock!"

As Raif turned, Heather grabbed his shoulder, twisted her knee behind his ankle, and tugged. A huge spew of water rose as he disappeared from view.

Heather stood there laughing, waiting for him to come up. He didn't.

Seconds passed. A full minute. "Raif, quit fooling around," Heather cried. "Where are you?"

There was no response. Had he had a heart attack? Had he hit his head on a submerged rock and knocked himself out? Really concerned, Heather took a deep breath and dived into the water, but she couldn't see any sign of Raif. She swam underwater for several yards, then surfaced and looked around her. No sign of him.

"Looking for me?" a voice asked behind her.

Heather whirled so swiftly that she nearly fell. He was standing inches behind her. "What were you doing?" she stammered.

"What was *I* doing? First you try to drown me, and then you start to yell, 'Where are you?'"

His mimicry of her voice was too much. She'd begun to laugh as he spoke, and soon she was shaking. Laughing too, he waded forward. Hanging on to each other for support, they laughed until they were weak. Heather's sides felt sore when she said, "You're evil, Raif Cornell. You knew very well I was worried about you. I thought you'd knocked yourself out and were floating helplessly under the water."

"So you were going to save me. Thank you for caring."

She started to say, "You're welcome," in the same bantering tone they'd been using but made the mistake of looking up at Raif.

Instantly, the lighthearted mood died. His eyes were shimmery with something besides merriment and soft with tenderness. Heather gave a little sound that was almost a protest before Raif's arms gathered her close.

This time there was no buildup. When Raif's mouth found hers, Heather was rocked by an explosion that seemed to turn solid ground to quicksand. Currents too strong for her to resist raced through her cool body, bringing it to fever heat.

And the temperature kept rising. While his mouth continued to explore hers, his hands strayed over her body, caressing her bare back, smoothing her barely-clothed hips. Now they were stroking upward over her waist and feeling their way over the delicate bones of her rib cage until they grazed the edge of her breasts.

Under the nudging insistence of his tongue, her lips parted. As his tongue explored the inner satin of her mouth, her own tongue tasted and touched. She could feel the pound of Raif's heart against her breasts, could hear his low, male growl of pleasure as he pulled her tight against his muscular hardness.

Heather's bones had begun to dissolve. Against that virile hardness and from the heat of her own blood, she had no protection. When Raif's hands roved downward, again caressing her ribs and waist, Heather pressed closer to him.

She'd never felt like this before. Never. It was almost as though she were drowning. Heather *wanted* to drown.

Only lack of oxygen drove them apart. Dazed, they blinked at each other. Raif drew a shaky breath and said huskily, "Oh, man."

Heather knew what he meant. She felt as though she'd survived an earthquake, and she couldn't catch her breath. Raif's kiss had turned her world upside down, totally destroyed her thinking process so that all she wanted was for him to kiss her again.

Obeying the wordless invitation in her eyes, Raif once again tightened his arms around Heather's waist. Almost involuntarily, her hands went up to clasp behind his neck. Wet, throbbing, barely clothed bodies slid together.

Suddenly, the raucous noise of a boom-box shattered the seething silence. Raif and Heather pulled apart and stared shoreward to see that they were no longer alone at Pine Lagoon.

"What's George doing here?" Raif exclaimed.

Chapter Four

"Obviously he's come for a swim," Heather said.

She felt as though she were fighting a losing battle with her body. Her muscles had gone slack, her pulse was galloping and, at this late date, alarm bells had started to sound inside her head. Given the weakened condition she was in, she was relieved that George had arrived.

"Let's ignore him," Raif suggested. "Maybe he'll go away."

"But he's waving at us," Heather pointed out.

Raif surrendered to the inevitable. "Then I'll race you back to shore. Last one in buys dinner."

He pushed off on the last word. "Hey, no fair," Heather sputtered indignantly as a powerful stroke sent him skimming away.

She was a good swimmer, but Raif was much more powerful. He stayed just ahead of her, but she suspected that he was holding himself in check, allowing her to almost catch up to him. Then at the last moment he would make a sudden spurt and leave her counting minnows.

One good turn deserved another. As they came within twenty yards of the shore, Heather gave a pitiful groan and sank beneath the surface.

In the few seconds it took him to catch on to her trick, she'd swam past him underwater and had taken the lead. "Make mine lobster," she shouted as she reached the shore a few feet ahead of him.

"You tricked me," he accused.

Heather laughed. "Don't try to welsh on a bet, mister."

She appealed to George, who nodded his shaggy head. "All's fair in love and food," he agreed.

"Whose side are you on, anyway?" As Heather walked up onto the beach, Raif hung back to admire how the wet bikini clung to her gently rounded curves. Heather's skin glowed with exercise, the flush of victory had warmed her cheeks, and the shadowed look he'd seen in her eyes earlier had completely disappeared. She looked vibrant and happy, and incredibly desirable.

His body's instant agreement made Raif literally stop and catch his breath. Heather heard that sharp intake and stopped walking. "Got a cramp?" she queried solicitously.

What ailed him wasn't a cramp and for sure it hadn't come from swimming. Silently, Raif cursed George's lousy timing.

"It's close to chow time back at the barn," he hinted. "Aren't you afraid the feeding machine will break down again?"

George nodded morosely. "It probably will."

"Then why desert the barnyard crew?" *And ruin a perfect moment?*

"The mail came."

With that, George plunged into the water. Heather, who'd wrapped her towel around herself, wondered, "What did he mean?"

"Beats me." As George emerged from the water, Raif shouted, "What mail?"

"Bills," he answered and disappeared again.

Raif shook his head, and Heather said, "It's high time I left."

"It's too early for egg pickup, and anyway, no one's minding the farm." Deliberately, Raif reached out and adjusted the towel around Heather. His hands lingered for a moment on her shoulders, and she could feel the warmth of his clasp seeking through the terry cloth through layers of skin and muscle and into her bones.

What was with her, anyway? With studied nonchalance, Heather bent down out of his reach and picked up a hairbrush from her picnic basket. "I need to be getting on. It's almost time to deliver Maggie's pies."

Frowning slightly, Raif said, "She should hire someone for that. Driving that cranky old pickup can't be a picnic."

"I'm glad to help Maggie. Mehitabel and I are used to each other. And as Maggie said just this morning, MM Pies is still a small operation."

"Think small and you'll stay small. You need to have vision." Raif sank down on the grass and watched Heather brush her hair into a cloud that sparkled with gold under the sun. Now *that* was a vision he could live with. His blood jolted with another resurgence of desire and then settled down to a pleasant, anticipatory pulsing. There were still a few days before he left for Boston, after all.

"About that dinner you say I owe you," he began.

She interrupted, "Don't try to put a guilt trip on me, mister. I won fair and square. I just followed the rules you set yourself." His eyebrows arched up, and the expression in his green eyes unnerved her. Heather had the feeling that he wasn't just looking at her but in her, reading her innermost thoughts. And right now she wasn't so sure that those thoughts were fit for mixed company.

Here was Raif sprawled out on the grass, looking like a centerfold in wet cutoffs that clung to his lean hips. A line of white below the waist contrasted sharply with his Florida tan. Any man that looked like that—big, indolent and yet with the leashed tension of a big cat about to spring—was a definite menace to susceptible females.

"And just what kind of rules do we set for this dinner?"

His deep voice was a tomcat's purr, and his eyes glowed with a warmth that she could almost feel. Heather's lips suddenly went dry, and she had trouble speaking casually. "I get to pick the restaurant, right?" He nodded. "Okay, then. We'll go to Rusty's."

Raif sat up and regarded her with horror. "You can't mean that shack on Main Street? The one that looks as if it should be closed by the Board of Health?"

"Oh, well. Being a tourist, you don't understand the facts of life."

"Wanna bet?"

"I mean, the facts of life in Mimosa." *No, idiot, you are not going to blush* she ordered herself. "Rusty's may be short on ambience, but their food is out of this world. You should try their soft-shell crab or their shrimp scampi. And their southern fried chicken will make your northern heart march to Dixie."

"Chicken. I never want to hear that word again."

Raif and Heather turned almost simultaneously to see that George had heaved himself out of the lagoon and was dripping all over the sand. "Chickens," George continued bitterly, "are a curse. They were created to plague mankind in general and me in particular."

"I gather that the bills were bad." Raif wanted to sound sympathetic, but his impatience must have shown, for George looked penitent.

"I'm sorry, old son. I didn't mean to rain on your parade." He stumped toward his towel and draped it around his waist, sarong style. "I'd better be getting back to the farm."

He looked so miserable that Heather felt sorry for him. "Is there something I can do?"

"Not unless you can tell me how to run Mountain Farm at a profit." George ruffled his hair until he resembled a thistle gone to seed. "Thanks for the good thoughts, though."

Heather could only nod sympathetically, but Raif asked, "Do you mean that?"

"Why not? I can use all the kind thoughts I can get."

"I mean, will you accept *my* help?" Raif's tone sharpened. "There's a way to turn things around, George. You could not only make yourself a profit but bring in serious money."

George said nothing, but his expression practically shouted, "Oh, yeah?" Heather tended to agree with him. After seeing Mountain Farm, she was sure that it would take an act of Congress to pull things together. No, she amended, make that an act of God.

"What with the cholesterol scare and the appearance of egg substitutes on the market, fresh eggs are losing ground." Raif paused before explaining, "Those were the findings of a market analysis Raifoods did last year when we were seriously thinking of branching into poultry."

"You're not telling me anything I don't already know, Raiford. What I need—"

"What you need, George, is a different angle."

Springing to his feet, Raif advanced purposefully on George. "Let's look at eggs as embryonic chickens. Now, chickens are becoming popular. Cholesterol-conscious people all over are switching from red meat to white. If you return to your original idea of breeding chickens, you can cash in on this trend."

George said something that sounded like, "Huh?"

"Think of it, George—a prototype breeding farm that'll set poultry men all over the country on their ears. The climate is right, the location is right, and the time is now." Striding forward, Raif clapped the big man on the shoulders. "I know you can do it."

Heather realized she'd been holding her breath. With the conviction in his voice and the new brilliance in his eyes, Raif was almost hypnotic.

But George was made of sterner stuff. "No, I can't," he retorted.

"I understand. You're talking finances. But with Raifoods to back you—" Raif broke off as George began to shake his head violently. "What? What's the matter with that?"

With a curious kind of dignity, George said, "I won't let you throw away your money. You're a good friend, Raiford, but I won't take advantage of your friendship."

"This has nothing to do with friendship. I told you we almost got into the poultry business but the timing wasn't right then. It is now. I'd never back a losing proposition, George. We'd both make money."

Completely forgotten, Heather felt as though she were watching a play unfold. George's eyes had begun to gleam, but he still shook his head.

"Go back to Boston and think it over. Set your people to making an analysis of the market. After that, if you still think Mountain Farm's worth your investment, we'll see."

"In a month," Raif said bluntly, "you'll be bankrupt."

Heather bit her lip as Raif continued, "if you want to go chapter eleven, there's nothing I can do for you."

It hurt Heather to see the pain in George's eyes. "It can't be that bad," she began.

As Raif glanced at her, Heather had the sense that she was looking at a stranger. Raif's eyes were preoccupied, almost impatient. The charming, laid-back man with whom she'd eaten and laughed and played in the water had completely disappeared.

She watched as Raif threw an arm around George's shoulders. "Let me tell you more about my thoughts for rebuilding a *new* Mountain Farm."

It was obvious that George's resistance was weakening. His big body quivered as he sighed. "And here I thought you were fishing and soaking up sun. When did you hatch the idea for this dream farm, anyway?"

"It's not a dream. It's a concept that can be turned into reality at a reasonable cost. Besides, I do my best thinking when I'm fishing." Raif's voice was satisfied, and so was his smile as he finally turned to Heather. "And speaking of fish, we have a dinner date. Are you free tonight, Heather?"

The smile was right, but the preoccupation in his tone told her that Raif's game plan had changed. His mind was now set squarely on the challenge of making George's farm successful. Heather could well believe that Raif had been thinking about eggs and chickens while he fished. After all, a true workaholic's brain never, ever shut down.

"Sorry, I need to help Maggie," she said. "Not to-night."

And not ever, she added silently. From this moment until he left for Boston, she was alert to danger. At all costs she was going to keep her distance from Mr. Cornell.

Once burned, twice shy.

Heather repeated that old saying to herself as she carried two nearly foot-high pies up the steps of the Proud Pelican Motel. On the top step she paused to wink at the enormous bronze replica of a pelican.

"Hiya, Perry," she quipped. "How's business?"

"So far so good." Norma Lighten, proprietor of the twenty-room motel, had opened the door for Heather. "Once it's built, though, that new motel on Route 19 is going to play merry hell with business."

Norma had bleached-blond hair and long red fingernails and she smoked a cigarillo in an ivory holder. Her accents were clipped, and her voice held the remnants of a Yankee twang. A transplanted New Englander, she'd come to Mimosa twenty years ago with her husband, Joe, had started the Pelican. Though she loved Mimosa fiercely, Norma still had ties with what she jokingly called "the cold and frozen north," and every year entertained a stream of guests-turned-friends from New England.

"Your clients would never leave you," Heather soothed. "They wouldn't dream of staying anyplace else but here at the Pelican."

"Maybe, maybe not. There's talk of a whole gym they're putting in that damned Cozee Motel, plus indoor pools and saunas.'' Norma nodded toward her own backyard where stooped-over Joe was cleaning the pool. ''At least those vultures won't have their place built before the Mimosa Fair. And talking of the fair, Maggie should get herself a booth. I know it's expensive, but it'd be a great place to sell pies.''

''We've been talking about it.'' Heather put Maggie's pies on the counter. ''I have the other three pies you ordered in Mehitabel. I'll bring them right up.''

''Tell Maggie I want five more. My guests loved the sample you sent, especially when I told them that they had Mr. Raiford Cornell's endorsement. Adela Sanglast was so impressed that she broke her diet and ordered a second piece of pie.''

Heather didn't like the little bump her heart gave at the sound of Raif's name. ''Oh?'' she said coolly.

''Avery was in here and told us about Raiford Cornell's having dinner with you guys. Heather, get a written endorsement from him. He's president of one of New England's biggest frozen-food companies.''

''If Raifoods is so big,'' Heather challenged, ''how come we haven't heard about him in Mimosa?''

''It's a New England company, that's why. According to Adela, she always buys the Raifoods brand because it's quality stuff.''

If Raif's coming to Mimosa had helped MM Pies, she was grateful. As Heather registered this thought, Norma said, ''I've seen him around town. Big, handsome dude. If I wasn't a married lady and twice his age, I'd go have my hair and nails done. What's he like, Heather? Avery said he saved you from an attack chicken.''

Avery was getting to be a pest. "He's nice enough," Heather said. "Now I'd better get those pies up here."

She went out the door almost at a run and raced down the steps. Once on the sidewalk, she asked herself what she was running from. Not Norma, whom she'd known almost all her life, and definitely not Raif.

She picked up two pies, thought about it, then balanced the third on her forearms. "Careful, Heather," she muttered. "Easy does it."

The kid on the skateboard came out of nowhere. One moment Heather was making for the Proud Pelican's steps, the next she had to jump back to avoid being hit. She managed to cling to two of the pies, but the third teetered precariously. Heather uttered a wail of anguish and closed her eyes as she felt the pie begin to fall.

There were running steps behind her and a deep voice exclaimed, "That was close. Lady, you almost had a casualty."

Heather's eyes popped open to see Raif straightening up with Maggie's third pie balanced in one hand. "You *saved* it," she breathed.

"I've caught some tough passes before, but this pie was almost history." Raif took a deep sniff. "Lemon and coconut—an interesting combination."

"Coco-Lemon Swirl is one of Norma Lighten's favorites." Heather's adrenaline had kicked into full gear, and her heart was pounding madly. "I shouldn't have tried to carry three at once, but I didn't see that kid."

"I thought Mimosa was a safe place, but now I'm not so sure. You're shaking like a leaf." Still carrying the rescued pie, he fell into step with her as she climbed the stairs. "You okay?"

"Sure I am." But Heather wasn't all that certain. She'd prided herself on keeping Raif out of her thoughts, but now she had to admit she'd been successful only because she hadn't had to deal with the reality of the man himself. She glanced at him out of the corners of her eyes and saw that he was wearing well-fitting slacks and an open-necked, pale blue shirt that showed off his terrific tan. The distinctive cologne he wore teased her nostrils with memories best forgotten.

Determined to deliver her pies, collect her check and leave as quickly as she could, Heather was foiled by Norma. The usually tough-minded owner of the Proud Pelican seemed to dissolve into putty when introduced to Raif. She fiddled with her cigarillo, fluttered her eyelashes and asked inane questions about Boston. "Just think," Norma gushed, "Mr. Cornell delivering Maggie's pies. Wait till I tell Adela."

"I won't ask who Adela is," Raif said when they'd finally made their escape.

"Wise man. Let's just say that you've made Maggie's pies even more desirable than ever," Heather told him.

"And that's very desirable." With those green eyes intent on her, Heather was suddenly conscious of the faded cotton shirt she'd tucked into her equally faded dungarees. "How is Maggie's business doing?" Raif continued.

"MM Pies is doing very well," she replied primly. "Thank you for your help, but now I've got to—wait a minute. Mehitabel's parked over there."

"But Rusty's is over here." Raif slid a big hand under the crook of Heather's elbow, guiding her down the street.

The orange warning light in Heather's brain snapped to red. "Hold it. I'm supposed to have lunch with Maggie. She's expecting me."

"Call her from the restaurant and tell her I'm paying a debt to society. I know the bet specified dinner, but somehow Rusty's looks less, ah, scary by daylight. At night, I have a feeling that unspeakable creatures crawl along the walls and lurk in the shadows."

Heather couldn't help chuckling, and Raif realized how much he'd missed that sound. He'd missed *her* during the past few days. He'd tried to phone her, but apparently Maggie had never heard of call-waiting, and his plan to drive down and see her had been foiled by all the work that had to be done at the farm.

In fact, he ought to be there right now. Surreptitiously, Raif glanced at his watch and wondered if he had time for lunch. Hell, he'd *make* time.

Heather was sure Raif had gone quiet because of Rusty's appearance. Seen from his eyes, it really had to look pretty unsavory—a big, square building with peeling plaster walls, a shingled roof that seemed about ready to collapse at any given moment, and dirty windows.

"Don't worry," she reassured him. "Nobody's ever gotten food poisoning here."

"There's always a first time." Raif winced as the screen door gave out a hideous screech, then glanced around the interior of the deserted restaurant. The floor looked as if it had been recently swept, and the rickety tables were covered with fresh paper table-cloths. However, instead of flower vases, each table boasted a roll of paper hand towels.

A lopsided sign taped to the cash register suggested they sit wherever they wished. Heather chose a table along the wall and Raif commented, "This can't be a popular spot with the lunch crowd."

"That's because we're early. By the time we've fin-ished eating, the place will be mobbed." She smiled brightly at the short, balding little man who came trotting up to them, and said, "Hi, Rusty. What's Myrna cooking today?"

The special of the day was seafood stew. Heather ordered it, but Raif asked to see the menu. "I'm the menu," Rusty replied. He rattled off a list of dishes, then paused to add that if he were Mr. Cornell, he'd order seafood stew. "You've never had anything like it in Boston," he said.

Raif's lips quirked as Rusty went away to bawl out his order. "It's amazing. I've been in Mimosa for just under two weeks, and everybody knows who I am."

"Does that bother you?"

"I'll admit it takes some getting used to. In Boston people tend to spend half their lives trying to make other people notice them." He paused to tear a hunk out of the loaf of bread Rusty had brought to their table. "I'll be damned. This is delicious bread."

"Homemade, of course. And it gets better," Heather promised.

She was right. The salad that had arrived with the bread was quite ordinary to look at but icy crisp and covered with a subtle, delicious dressing. As for the seafood stew, it was thick with crayfish, shrimp, crab and fish.

"Remind me never to judge a restaurant by its roof again," Raif said, blissfully munching away. "This stuff is fabulous."

A warm glow had taken possession of Heather. "Glad to hear it. You were so quiet I thought you were eating just to be polite."

Raif tore off another hunk of the bread and soaked up the remaining gravy in his bowl. "People in Boston would kill for this stuff."

He looked miles away from the business tycoon she'd last seen at Pine Lagoon, but mention of his hometown brought Heather up short. "Weren't you supposed to be leaving day before yesterday?"

"Since George and I are going into partnership, I've lengthened my stay." Looking slightly guilty, Raif added, "I've meant to come over and tell you about it, Heather, but things have been rather hectic lately."

As he spoke the front door screeched open and half a dozen men in work clothes clomped in. At their heels came three well-dressed old ladies, a young couple holding hands, and several young matrons with their toddlers in tow.

"The lunch crowd arrives," Heather explained, then groaned. At the tail end of the crowd was Avery Lewis, together with several men in business suits.

In an hour, everyone in Mimosa would know Heather Leigh had had lunch with Raif Cornell. Perhaps he wouldn't spot her, but of course he did. "Heather," Avery chirruped. "I thought I saw Mehitabel parked t'other side of the street."

He started over to their table, saw Raif and seemed to freeze in his tracks. Then, with an audible sniff, he turned his back on them. As the little accountant stomped off to the table his companions had chosen, Heather exclaimed, "What in the world's gotten into him?"

"Avery evidently doesn't approve of New Mountain Farm."

Heather repeated, "*New* Mountain Farm?" and watched a self-satisfied expression filter down over Raif's face.

"I had a team of my people fly down to do a market analysis. Their preliminary reports have got even George convinced that our joint venture will work."

She hadn't seen him for a few days and already he'd had his team flown in to analyze the market. Mr. Cornell certainly moved fast.

"So you're going ahead with your plans," she heard herself say. "You're going to finance Mountain Farm."

"*New* Mountain Farm," he corrected. "As a matter of fact, I'm in town to pick up some documents we need for a meeting with the builders."

Builders?

"Perhaps you've heard of Simonson and Sons from Clearwater?" She shook her head and he added, "You'll know the architectural firm I've engaged, though—Leonard Mannering. They're local, have an excellent reputation, and their work has the contemporary flair I'm after.'' Raif glanced at his watch, adding, ''They'll all be at the farm in an hour.''

The absorbed look in his eyes reminded Heather of a day last spring when she and Bill had taken a walk in the hills. She'd been lost in the beauty of the day, and she'd thought Bill felt the same way until he told her that he'd just solved a problematic layout that had nagged him for a week, and would she mind not having dinner tonight because he wanted to get the idea down while it was still fresh?

Naturally, Raif had been quiet as he ate. He'd probably been wondering how well Rusty's seafood stew froze.

All the good food that Heather had consumed seemed to bunch into a tight knot in her stomach. As she pushed the remainder of her lunch away from her, Raif protested, ''Woman, it's sinful to leave that.''

It was a sin that his eyes were the color of spring leaves, that his smile could melt a snowbank and that his deep voice could persuade or cajole or caress. Yet Heather knew this was all window dressing. Under that handsome exterior beat a ticker tape instead of a heart.

She glanced at Avery and noted that the accountant was staring at Raif. He looked as if he'd swallowed a lemon.

Usually Heather didn't see eye to eye with Avery, but this time they were in sync. Avery was wishing that Mr. Cornell would go back to Boston and leave Mimosa alone, and Heather agreed with all her heart.

Chapter Five

Mehitabel creaked, clanked and groaned as she toiled up the slope to Mountain Farm, but for once Heather's ear wasn't tuned to the old pickup's ailments. Half her mind was on Maggie's breakfast-table decision that she was going to rent a booth at the upcoming Mimosa Fair and never mind the cost. The other half kept coming back to Raif Cornell.

She hadn't seen Raif since their lunch at Rusty's three days ago, and during that time she'd kept busy helping Maggie. Now she'd be busier still. In the week they had left before the fair, she'd have to design an eye-catching sign for Maggie's booth, get name cards printed up and order more leaflets and brochures from the printers.

Heather's thoughts trailed off as a truck came lumbering down the narrow gravel path toward her. She turned Mehitabel's wheel sharply to avoid a collision and then stared as an earth mover lurched down the slope.

What in the world was going on? As Mehitabel reluctantly crested the hill, Heather exclaimed, "Oh, *wow.*"

George's once-laid-back farm was a hotbed of activity. The land adjacent to the laying house had been cleared by bulldozers, piles of lumber and gravel were neatly stacked by the farmhouse, and a team of surveyors was at work.

Heather looked around for Raif or George and found them standing together with two other men and a woman, on high ground behind the farmhouse. Raif was gesturing energetically.

Perhaps she should return another time. But as if he'd intercepted her thought, Raif glanced her way. When he saw Mehitabel, he waved a greeting, spoke briefly with his companions and came striding toward her.

"I'm glad you're here," he called.

The pleasure in his eyes was genuine, but *once bitten, twice shy,* she reminded herself sternly.

"I didn't mean to interrupt you," she said. "I just came by for Maggie's eggs and to drop off the sign you ordered for George."

He looked blank for a moment and then said, "Oh, right, the sign." Then, opening the pickup's door, he held out a hand to help her descend. "How have you been? I've missed you, Heather."

She despised herself for reacting to the way his deep voice caressed her name. His touch was sending tendrils of warmth curling through her veins, and she hastily freed her hand. "I'm fine," she said. "And I see you've been busy."

"There's a lot to do. The ground has to be leveled, and the road to the farm needs to be widened so that the builder's machinery can have access." He paused. "I meant to stop by and see you, but it's been hectic. How's Maggie these days?"

"She's finally decided to go for the big time and rent a booth at the Mimosa Fair."

The patronizing way in which Raif said, "Aha," raised Heather's hackles.

"I gather that you haven't heard about our fair?" she challenged.

He looked vague. "I think George mentioned it. The great event takes place in early February, doesn't it?"

"A week from today. And it really *is* a big event. It's one of the big attractions hereabouts and folks from all over Florida, and as far as Louisiana and Virginia, in fact, have been coming to Mimosa Fair for years." Raif still didn't look impressed so she added, "They wouldn't miss it for the world."

"Just where is this fair held?"

His eyebrow had quirked up. He looked quizzical, faintly amused. Obviously he considered himself above such bucolic festivities.

"In the big park at the other end of town," she said coldly. "It's not just a two-bit local fair, Raif. Merchants from all over Florida bring their wares to demonstrate or sell, politicians make an appearance and every special-interest group you can shake a stick at has a booth. There's a flea market and an antique car show, and the 4-H clubs show their stuff. There's a huge parade that heads down Main Street and ends up at the park to start the festivities. And of course there's the dance on Saturday night.''

"Which is held in the Mimosa High School gym, naturally.''

Defensively, Heather retorted, "It's a great place for a dance.''

Ignoring Raif's grin, Heather reached into her pickup and pulled out a large wooden sign.

"Here's the sign you ordered,'' she said somewhat stiffly. "Since the name of the farm has changed, I put New Mountain Farm on it. Is that satisfactory?''

Raif examined the sign before nodding. "Excellent. Now our workers will be able to find us without calling the highway patrol. I'll put it up right away.'' He added, "If you'll come up to the house, I'll write you a check for your work.''

"I'd rather be paid in eggs,'' Heather said. "I've been too busy to come by the last few days, and we're running low. I doubt if we can make do just on the broken ones today.''

She started toward the laying house, but he stopped her. "I need to talk to you, Heather. Please come to the house for a moment.''

Maggie had her hands full and needed her to help. She had to run down to the office of the *Mimosa Herald* and make sure that her ads for MM Pies were in the latest edition. Excuses swirled through Heather's mind, but instead she asked, "What do you want to talk about?''

Tucking a hand through her arm, Raif drew her up the path toward the farmhouse. As they walked, she could hear George shouting something to one of the surveyors.

"You've done a lot in a short time," she exclaimed.

"We're operating on a tight time frame. I want to make sure that the building construction is going smoothly before I leave for Boston."

"And when will that be?" she asked. Casually, she hoped.

"That depends on a lot of things." He gave the arm he held a little squeeze, then pushed the screen door open. "Come on in and I'll explain."

Inside, the farmhouse looked messier than ever. Maps and plans were stacked everywhere, and Groucho had a demented look. Heather picked her way around and through the confusion until Raif stopped at what she supposed might be the dining-room table.

"These are our architect's blueprints for New Mountain Farm," he said.

She wasn't prepared for the stir of excitement she felt as she looked down at the blueprints. What Raif envisioned for George's new farm was modern and pleasing to the eye. The two central buildings held her attention with their clean, spare lines.

Raif said, "On consideration, we've decided to keep the egg business going, so we have two laying houses. One is for egg production and the second for breeder fowls. The way the houses are constructed—they're called high rises because of their height—will emphasize cleanliness, efficiency and good working conditions."

"Working conditions for the chickens?"

She'd asked the question in jest, but he answered quite seriously, "Healthy fowls produce superior eggs. They won't be cramped into cages but allowed free run within their own sectors. Each sector will contain a harem of a dozen hens and a rooster. Food will be strictly monitored, since there's evidence that diet can reduce the cholesterol content of eggs, and will be dispensed automatically by computer."

Raif explained how the eggs produced by the breeding fowls would roll onto a conveyor belt, would be sorted, graded and placed into temperature-controlled storage to await pickup by firms that would incubate and hatch the eggs. "If New Mountain Farm is as successful as I feel it'll be, Raifoods will eliminate the middleman in a few years. We'll acquire an incubating plant and raise our own chickens for market."

His enthusiasm was contagious. "I think you've done it," Heather exclaimed. "You've turned a turkey into a goose that'll lay golden eggs."

"I'm glad you think so because I need you to translate these concepts for the public." She looked up at him questioningly and he added, "I want to hire you to help me publicize New Mountain Farm."

"Now, wait a minute." Heather put up her hands, palms out, as if to ward off attack. "I don't think you realize what you're saying."

Raif leaned against the wall and folded his arms across his broad chest. "No?"

He looked like a man who knew exactly what he wanted and how to get it, but Heather wasn't about to be intimidated.

"There's no way that I could give you the scope you'd need to promote something like this," she told him. "You need a large, established agency. I'm sure your architects will be able to recommend—"

"You misunderstand," he interrupted. "I certainly don't mean that you're to take on New Mountain Farm's promo single-handed. Raifoods has its own advertising and promotion department, and we've got some very talented artists."

"Then why did you just say—"

Again he interrupted. "Because my people are in Boston, and you're here. You know Mimosa and can sense intangibles that an out-of-towner couldn't. I want to hire you to do a series of designs of New Mountain Farm. My staff can then base their finished work on them."

"That's very flattering." Heather felt a touch of regret as she added, "Unfortunately, it wouldn't work. I know you'll want them immediately, and just now I'm up to my ears with helping Maggie."

"I'm sure we can arrange a mutually satisfactory solution and besides, we haven't discussed money." Raif casually named a sum that took her breath away, and while she was getting back her equilibrium he added, "We could get together and work on some preliminary sketches this evening. No, that won't do. I've got a meeting with the builder. At two o'clock tomorrow afternoon?"

He was sure of himself, and why shouldn't he be? He knew that she couldn't afford to turn down a well-paying job and he also knew that she was intrigued with his concepts. As Heather bent over the blueprints once again, ideas began to crowd into her head. She felt the thrill of challenge.

"Two o'clock, then?" Raif repeated.

"That would be fine." She looked up at him as she spoke and saw an intensity in his green eyes that astonished her.

Was all that fervor and enthusiasm for New Mountain Farm? But of course it was. Workaholics *really* could get into their work.

Since Raif had a business lunch on Saturday afternoon, they agreed to hold their meeting at Maggie's. He arrived promptly at two and found Heather waiting for him on the porch.

Without wasting time she ushered him into Maggie's rather formal dining room. Here the long, polished oak table had been set with sketch pad, pens, colored markers and a portfolio.

"Coffee?" Heather asked. "Maggie made a fresh pot before she left. She's had a standing appointment at Darlene's Beauty Spot every Saturday afternoon at two o'clock for the last thirty years. I think Darlene would call the police if Maggie ever missed an appointment. She'd be afraid something dreadful had happened."

Why was she babbling like this? Heather wondered. Nerves, of course. She'd promised herself that this meeting would be held along the high professional lines that Raif undoubtedly set for his staff. The man was paying top dollar for her services, and she meant to deliver.

"Coffee?" she repeated, but Raif shook his head.

"Lunch nearly did me in. Coffee would finish me off."

"Where did you go?" He told her, and Heather groaned. "That explains it. Only snobs and visiting bigwigs go to the Mandalay. It's overpriced, the waiters sneer at you, and the food is so rich it gives you indigestion for a month."

Raif looked as though he agreed. "It was Jim Baxter's idea," he said.

Heather pricked up her ears. "You had lunch with our mayor?"

"With him and many of the other big wheels in town." Raif paused to explain. "After Avery cut me dead at Rusty's, I thought I'd better get Mimosa's big guns together and show them what New Mountain Farm could do for Mimosa's economy. More jobs, more prestige, more tax money. That was what I was selling."

Heather poured herself a cup of coffee. "I hope you didn't invite Avery."

"Sure I did." Raif grinned reminiscently. "He got really eloquent about traffic tie-ups and problems with the environment. Then he had two martinis and accused me of being a bossy Yankee who thought I could come down south and push people around."

Heather couldn't help laughing as she pictured Avery delivering this last speech. "Did he ever calm down?"

"Eventually, but that's not why I invited him. Avery realizes now that very few people agree with him. He's also had his say in public, and that should satisfy him." Idly, Raif reached for Heather's portfolio and flipped it open. "I like the watercolor you've done from that sketch of Pine Lagoon."

"I forgot that was in there." Setting down her coffee cup, Heather took the watercolor away and drew out a dozen sketches. "These are roughs, of course, but I've experimented with different ideas. This meeting is really a shopping expedition, Raif. Together we can decide in which direction you want to go."

That statement was definitely open to misinterpretation. As Raif examined the sketches she set before him, he was very aware of Heather's nearness. She was standing so close behind his chair that her subtle, rose-and-sunshine scent seemed to surround him.

With an effort, he concentrated on the business at hand. "I like what you've done here," he told her, "but it's not quite the image I want to project."

Heather listened intently to his suggestions, then sat down beside him, flipped her sketch pad open and drew swiftly. "Is this more what you had in mind?"

As he leaned over to take a better look, his cheek brushed her hair. The soft curls seemed to caress his skin.

"Do you like this better?" Heather was asking.

What he *really* would like was to gather Heather into his arms. He wanted to crush her warm softness to him and kiss the generous curve of her lips. No woman, Raif thought disjointedly, had the right to have a mouth like that. It was curved into a sweet shape that seemed to whisper, "Kiss me."

Dimly, he was aware that Heather was speaking. Something about using space to make its own statement. "Try it," he said. "Let me see what you mean."

As she bent forward to work, he could distinguish the curve of her breasts. Even though they were hidden by the businesslike blouse she was wearing, he remembered vividly how her curves had filled out a bikini.

Was he catching a cold that he had to keep clearing his throat? Heather glanced up at Raif and met a look that could have set an ice cube on fire. He looked as he'd done when they were both in the water and he'd taken her into his arms to kiss her. The memory of his mouth on hers, the press of his hard, bare chest against hers was so vivid that Heather shivered.

"How's it coming?" Raif hoped that his voice didn't sound as disjointed as he felt.

Heather knew that he was on fire with enthusiasm for his new business venture—New Mountain Farm. She tried to fix her mind on her work, but his nearness made concentration difficult, and her hands had become unsteady.

"I can't work with you looking over my shoulder," she protested.

The feeling was mutual. He'd forgotten just how deeply Heather could affect him. Almost glad of the excuse to put some distance between them, Raif got to his feet and began to walk about the dining room, examining the prints on the walls and the photographs.

The first of these was an enlarged snapshot of a pretty young woman, a good-looking young man, and a little girl with long braids down either side of her smiling face—Heather with her late parents. There were also photos of Heather with Maggie and a big, smiling man who had to be Sam, a close-up of Heather at her graduation, and one recent one of her smiling up at a good-looking guy with good teeth and expensively coiffured blond hair.

"A friend from New York?" Raif wondered.

Heather glanced up from her sketch pad. "What? Oh, that's Bill Reese, my ex-fiancé. We used to work together."

Her *ex*-fiancé. Raif wasn't prepared for the stab of relief he felt, and the less definable emotion that followed as it occurred to him that Bill Reese could have put those shadows in Heather's eyes.

Someone like Heather would invest a lot of herself into a relationship, and no doubt Teeth-and-Hair had somehow betrayed her trust. Raif was still frowning over this thought when Heather turned her sketchbook around. "What do you think of this concept?"

As he walked back to the table he asked casually, "Does he still work for P. and L.?"

"Bill? Oh, yes. He was promoted to vice president of our design department before Thanksgiving. He's very talented, very smart."

"And hardworking, trustworthy and reverent," Raif concluded. It was astonishing how much he disliked the man, and his words were more clipped than usual as he said, "Okay, let me see what you've done."

Heather watched him anxiously as he studied her sketch. He was scowling, and his mouth was a tight, hard line. "If that's not where you'd like to be, I can try something completely different," she said.

But Raif shook his head. It had taken an effort to turn his attention from Heather to the business at hand, but now that he'd looked over her sketch he was definitely impressed. Heather had taken his suggestions and transformed them into an original idea that was better than anything he'd envisioned.

"It's what I wanted," he exclaimed. "With the right copy, this idea will be dynamite."

Heather beamed, then gasped as he swung her chair around, grasped her hands in his and pulled her to her feet and into his arms. "I knew we'd work well together," Raif cried. "Dammit, Heather, you're too rare to lose. I can't let you get away."

Deep within her, Heather's heart was starting to do a meltdown. No use denying facts—she'd really missed Raif's arms around her. She'd missed the hard feel of his body pressed against hers, his scent, everything about him.

"Was I going someplace?" she managed.

"I don't want to leave for Boston without you," Raif continued. "I want you to come with me."

Joy, so strong as to be almost painful, lanced through her. For one unthinking moment happiness without form or conscious thought sent her skimming over the moon. But Raif was still talking.

"I've always thought you were wasted here in Mimosa," he was saying. "You've got skill, imagination, and most important of all you can take suggestions and incorporate them in your own vision. Believe me, you'd fit right in with my team."

Heather felt as though she'd been slapped in the face. He was offering her a *job*.

And what else did you think he wanted from you, ninny? Stung by the sneering voice inside her brain, Heather took a step backward, fetched up against a chair and carefully lowered herself into it.

"I don't think I'd like Boston," she heard herself say.

Green eyes narrowed. "Have you ever been there?"

"Twice, actually. I attended a trade show once, and another time Bill and I flew down to meet with one of P. and L.'s accounts." He seemed about to protest, so she said decisively, "I like it here in Mimosa, Raif. I mean to stay here."

Methinks the lady doth protest too much—came into Raif's mind but Heather seemed totally sincere. She meant what she said, or at least she thought she did. "Because Maggie needs you?" Raif prodded.

"Sure, but that's not the only reason."

She was getting defensive. As an experienced negotiator, Raif knew that it was time to back off. "Perhaps you'd just like to visit Raifoods once, no strings attached," he suggested. His voice softened as he added, "Boston isn't all work and trade shows, Heather. It's the Charles at sunset. It's music. It's the swan boats in the garden and Celtic games and succulent lobsters dripping with butter. I'd like to show it all to you."

His deep voice was a caress. The air pulsed with his presence, with the clean, vital masculine scent that was uniquely his. Her sense of balance and common sense collapsed, and for a moment Heather pictured herself with Raif in Boston. Sailing on the Charles at sunset. Listening to the Pops. Strolling through the spring flowers. Working with him . . .

Once bitten, twice shy.

Heather ran her tongue over her dry lips. "Your offer is flattering," she said, "but I still like Mimosa." Conviction strengthened her voice as she added, "Here, people take time out to smell the flowers."

"Very nice, if you happen to like flowers." She drew back involuntarily as he reached out, but he only tapped her sketchbook with his finger. "I'd like to see completed designs along these lines. Could you bring them up to the farm tomorrow?"

Tomorrow was Sunday, but there would be no day of rest for someone like Raif. "You've got it," Heather said crisply. "What time?"

"It doesn't matter. I plan to be working all day."

Leaning away from the document that had absorbed his attention for the past few hours, Raif stretched his back to ease a crick that had formed at the base of his spine. The revised contract seemed to be airtight, so why did he have this odd feeling of unease?

Perhaps it was an overreaction to the delays incurred as they had hashed and rehashed minor points in the contract. Perhaps it was because he was here and not in Boston.

The more
you love romance . . .
the more
you'll love this offer

FREE!

*Mail this
heart today!
(see inside)*

**Join us on a Silhouette® Honeymoon
and we'll give you
4 free books
A free Victorian picture frame
And a free mystery gift**

IT'S A
SILHOUETTE HONEYMOON—
A SWEETHEART OF A FREE OFFER!
HERE'S WHAT YOU GET:

1. Four New Silhouette Romance™ Novels—FREE!

Take a Silhouette Honeymoon with your four exciting romances—yours FREE from Silhouette Reader Service™. Each of these hot-off-the-press novels brings you the passion and tenderness of today's greatest love stories . . . your free passports to bright new worlds of love and foreign adventure.

2. Lovely Victorian Picture Frame— FREE!

This lovely Victorian pewter-finish miniature is perfect for displaying a treasured photograph. And it's yours FREE as added thanks for giving our Reader Service a try!

3. An Exciting Mystery Bonus—FREE!

You'll be thrilled with this surprise gift. It is useful as well as practical.

4. Free Home Delivery!

Join the Silhouette Reader Service™ and enjoy the convenience of pre-viewing 6 new books every month delivered right to your home. Each book is yours for only $2.25* each. And there is no extra charge for postage and handling. It's a sweetheart of a deal for you! If you're not completely satisfied, you may cancel at anytime, for any reason, simply by sending us a note or shipping statement marked "cancel" or by re-turning any shipment to us at our cost.

5. Free Insiders' Newsletter!

You'll get our monthly newsletter, packed with news about your favorite writers, upcoming books, even recipes from your favorite authors.

6. More Surprise Gifts!

Because our home subscribers are our most valued readers, when you join the Silhouette Reader Service™, we'll be sending you additional free gifts from time to time—as a token of our appreciation.

START YOUR SILHOUETTE HONEYMOON TODAY—JUST COM-PLETE, DETACH AND MAIL YOUR FREE-OFFER CARD

*Terms and prices subject to change without notice. Sales tax applicable in NY.

Get your fabulous gifts ABSOLUTELY FREE!

MAIL THIS CARD TODAY.

DETACH AND MAIL TODAY!

GIVE YOUR HEART TO SILHOUETTE

Yes! Please send me my four Silhouette Romance® novels FREE, along with my free Victorian picture frame and free mystery gift. I wish to receive all the benefits of the Silhouette Reader Service™ as explained on the opposite page.

NAME _____
(PLEASE PRINT)

ADDRESS _____ APT. _____

CITY _____ STATE _____

ZIP CODE _____

215 CIS ACET
(U-SIL-R-01/91)

PLACE
HEART STICKER
HERE

SILHOUETTE READER SERVICE™ "NO-RISK" GUARANTEE

—There's no obligation to buy—and the free gifts remain yours to keep.

—You receive books months before they appear in stores.

—You may end your subscription anytime by sending us a note or shipping statement marked "cancel" or by returning any shipment to us at our cost.

START YOUR
SILHOUETTE HONEYMOON TODAY.
JUST COMPLETE, DETACH AND MAIL YOUR
FREE-OFFER CARD.

If offer card below is missing write to:
Silhouette Reader Service, 3010 Walden Ave.,
P.O. Box 1867, Buffalo, NY 14269-1867.

BUSINESS REPLY MAIL

FIRST CLASS MAIL   PERMIT NO. 717   BUFFALO, NY

POSTAGE WILL BE PAID BY ADDRESSEE

SILHOUETTE READER SERVICE
3010 WALDEN AVE
PO BOX 1867
BUFFALO NY 14240-9952

NO POSTAGE
NECESSARY
IF MAILED
IN THE
UNITED STATES

DETACH AND MAIL TODAY!

Mimosa was hardly a hub of industry or efficiency. Raif was actually grateful that he'd tracked down a fax machine and thus obtained the revised contract without loss of time. They'd lost enough of that valuable commodity already and, dammit, he needed Swiftee if he was going to expand Raifoods' New Jersey market.

Raif got up from his chair and walked out onto the porch. It was early afternoon, and the warm sun beat down on the unassembled materials of the laying houses. It bothered him that there was no work going on today. With the tight time frame they were on, the builder should be working overtime.

But this was Mimosa, where people stopped to smell the flowers. In many ways, Raif thought, getting back home would be a relief. He'd be back in the mainstream again, associating with people who thought as he did. Here in Mimosa the contractors from Clearwater turned down overtime pay in order to race stock cars, or work on boats, or lie out in the sun with a couple of cool ones. Even George made it plain that it was unpatriotic to work on a Sunday.

Accordingly, today he'd hired someone to collect his eggs, and he'd gone fishing. "You should come with me, old son," George had said. "Too much work makes a man's brain go limp, not to mention certain other vital parts. I'll take the car and leave you the pickup in case you see the light."

Raif frowned. Sometimes he wondered if George had the drive, the determination and the discipline to make a success of New Mountain Farm. Perhaps once he actually saw designs of the place, he'd snap to.

And speaking of designs... Raif glanced at his watch and swore under his breath. Where was Heather, anyway? He'd tried to phone her earlier, but the line had been busy as usual. He was about to try the number again when he heard the distinctive noise of Mehitabel laboring up the slope.

In a moment, the ancient pickup nosed itself over the top of the slope, and Raif's frown became one of concern. Heather needed to get herself more reliable transportation. That tub of nuts and bolts didn't look safe to drive.

As though in response to his thought, Mehitabel gave a lurch, swung violently to the left and then to the right, skidded off the gravel road and careened into a tree.

"Heather!"

Raif was down the steps and running even before the dull thud of the collision registered in his brain. "Heather," he shouted again, as he raced toward the pickup.

He found her slumped over in her safety belt. Her hands were still gripping the steering wheel, and as Raif reached in to click off the ignition, she stirred.

"Wha-what are you doing?"

Snapping the lock of the safety belt, Raif gathered her into his arms. She seemed incredibly light, and her bones were fragile against him. With horror he saw that there was a darkening bruise on her forehead.

"Are you all right?" he demanded. "Heather, what happened?"

She'd been driving Mehitabel, and then suddenly there'd been this grinding lurch and then the impact, and she'd bumped her head. "My fault," Heather muttered. "I should have pulled maintenance. I'll bet my boots it was the front right tie-rod end."

Hushing her, Raif began to stride toward the farmhouse. "Don't talk. I'm going to take you to the house and call a doctor. You may have a concussion."

She protested. "I'm fine, Raif. Put me down."

"Not a chance." He strode up the front steps, kicked open the screen door and lowered her gently onto the couch. Kneeling before her, he then probed the bruise on her forehead. She winced. "Hurts?"

"Naturally it hurts. I banged my head."

"Do you have double vision?" Raif insisted.

She could see only one of him, but that one image was disquieting enough. He looked worried sick, and in the green eyes that were so close to hers she saw an upside-down reflection of herself. That was the effect he had on her, she thought dazedly. Whenever Raif was around, she never knew whether she was standing on her feet or on her head.

She had to put some space between them, pronto. Heather bolted upright on the couch and said sternly, "Read my lips—I'm fine." She started to get up, but Raif pushed her down again.

"I'm going to call a doctor."

"On Sunday? Even in Mimosa doctors take the day off."

"Then I'll drive you to a hospital. You need to be X-rayed." She shook her head, and he exploded, "Don't be so stubborn. I thought you'd been badly hurt. And when I saw you slumped over the wheel, I was afraid..."

His words trailed away as Raif was hit by a terror that he could hardly bear to put into words. "I thought I'd lost you," he whispered, and reaching out almost blindly, he gathered her into his arms.

Chapter Six

The fit was exactly right. Heather's slender, compact body nestled against Raif as if she'd been created especially for that purpose. His arms cradled her as though they'd been tailor-made to shield her. Her softness and his hardness melded perfectly.

Meanwhile their lips were doing their own melding. The intensity of this kiss jarred them both free from their moorings and catapulted them into a universe where none of the old rules made sense. Heather's reasoning powers disappeared into the woodwork as Raif's mouth captured hers, and when his tongue purposefully nudged her lips apart, she surrendered to its marauding caresses. His exploration of her inner mouth started a storm building within her.

"Heather," Raif whispered. "Beautiful Heather." Punctuating his words with small, passionate kisses, he sank down beside her on the couch. "You don't know how much I've wanted to do this."

His lips left hers to brush shadow kisses across her jawline, her temples, her chin. "And this."

The moist heat of his tongue laved the hollow of her throat. His hands stroked her shoulders, traced erotic designs on her back. Involuntarily, her own hands began to rove on their own, sliding over the smooth muscles of his forearms up to his shoulders and neck, up farther to the crispy silk of his hair.

"You taste like wine and honey and roses." Raif's words were an indistinct mutter against her as his mouth roved to the V of her blouse. Impatiently, his lips nudged away the fabric as it sought the beginning curve of her breast.

The storm inside Heather crested and broke as Raif's mouth brushed her still-clothed nipple. "Raif, don't—" But she broke off in confusion. She hadn't the least idea whether she wanted him to stop or go on.

Some deep-rooted instinct of self-preservation in Heather's brain came alive and warned her to stop all this before she went totally out of control. This was crazy. She didn't want this to happen. She'd planned for it not to happen. She didn't want to get involved with Raif.

But the urgent warnings shut down as Raif's mouth found hers again. When his lips settled against hers, her mouth parted in immediate surrender. Their tongues touched, caressed, and she breathed with the oxygen from his lungs. It was almost as though he were a part of her, interwoven with her somehow. She couldn't get enough of his kisses or of the touch of his hands.

Those hands were evoking erotic magic as they smoothed her back, curved down over the line of her hips and thighs. Liquid heat followed his touch, spiraling through her veins and draining the last of her resistance.

Now he lay back on the couch. Gently tugging her down with him, he drew her over him so that her softness was pressed against his length. A hard-muscled leg slid between hers, and Heather was joltingly, acutely conscious of his virile need of her.

And she needed him. Her breasts were as heavy as ripe fruit, and her body strained against the confines of her clothing.

In an unthinking attempt to do away with the barrier of silk and cotton, she slid her hand between the buttons of his shirt. The texture and warmth of his skin recalled that day at Pine Lagoon, and the craving she felt for the feel of his bare flesh against her was unbearable.

As though intuiting her desire, Raif reached down. He tugged her blouse free from the waistband of her slacks and slipped his hands under the cloth. The silky skin of her back felt fevered against his palm, and through her blouse and his shirt he could feel the pounding of her heart. Bemused as he was, the thought registered: she wanted him as much as he wanted her.

Raif's muscle and sinew, blood and bone had fused together into one searing need. That need became near-frenzy as he continued to kiss Heather with a single-minded intensity. He caressed her back and abdomen, the ridges of her ribs, the proud curve of her breast.

Desire so great that she could hardly bear it lanced through Heather. The storm was building force again, and she knew that this time it would pull her under. A few more seconds and she'd be out of manageable waters and be whirled away into the darkness and the storm.

Heather couldn't keep back a moan as she felt Raif's hand leave her breast, slide up her back to the closure of her bra. The moment was now. She could stop him and herself, or she could—

Dimly, Heather realized that Raif's body language had changed. The arms that held her were rigid with a tension that was different from the passionate hunger of a second ago. But before her fuzzy thoughts could clear, he drew away from her and examined her face anxiously.

"Did I hurt you?" he was asking.

"N-no." But Heather's voice cracked on the word, and his eyes narrowed. Carefully, as though he were handling a cut-glass vase, he lifted her and himself to a sitting position on the couch.

"You need to go to a doctor," he told her.

I thought we already were playing doctor. The inane thought flashed into Heather's mind, leaving her with a crazy urge to giggle. She had to do something to ease the emotions raging through her body. She ached, her breasts felt sore and her head was spinning—but not from that bump that Raif seemed so worried about.

"Do you want some water?" Raif was asking.

What she wanted was for him to take her back in his arms. Hastily, Heather scooted some distance away from him.

"I'm okay," she told him. "I'm really fine." She tried for a smile as she added, "Look, I have a hard head. One time when I was pulling maintenance on Mehitabel, the hood came down on my head and nearly knocked me out. Sam said anyone else would have ended up in the hospital."

He frowned. "That pickup's a death trap. You have to get rid of it."

"Getting rid of Mehitabel would be like killing off a member of the family. It was my fault for being too busy to give her a real overhaul." Heather stood up and ran her hands through her hair. "And, talking of Mehitabel, the sketches are on the front seat. If you'll go get them, I'll call Eddy Simms at the Big S. Eddy's open on Sunday. He'll send a tow."

But Raif was shaking his head. "First I want to make sure you're okay. Head injuries can be dangerous."

While she argued, he hustled her out of doors and into his pickup. Resignedly, Heather gave him directions to the nearest hospital in a town twenty miles away. "Twenty miles, for Pete's sake," Raif exploded. "What happens if there's an emergency?"

He certainly acted as though *she* were an emergency. Heather was embarrassed at the fuss that Raif made when they got to the hospital, insisting that X rays be taken and quizzing the resident on duty. "Are you sure you don't want to keep her for observation?'' he demanded when the doctor said she could go home.

The resident, an unflappable young woman, bore Raif's inquisition calmly, but when he'd gone out to bring the pickup around to the door, she gave Heather a conspiratorial wink. "You're fine, but he won't believe it. He'll wait on you hand and foot for the rest of the day, and my professional advice is to enjoy it while it lasts. Believe me, he'll soon be back to normal."

Heather wished that "soon" would hurry up and come. When Raif wanted to help her into the pickup, she complained. "Will you please stop fussing over me? I'm not an invalid. What's got into you, anyway?"

You, he almost said. *You've gotten under my skin, Heather Leigh.* Instead, he gave her one of his swift grins. "You're acting mean. That definitely means that I have to watch you."

"Says who?"

"People with concussions often exhibit personality disorders." Seeing Heather's eyes narrow ominously, he added, "Since you hurt yourself while you were bringing me those sketches, I feel responsible. I'll feel better if we stay together at least until we've had some dinner."

"It's only three o'clock," Heather retorted, but the mention of food had done its damage. She'd worked on the drawings until late last night and again this morning, and in order to get the renderings exactly right, she'd skipped lunch. Her stomach, reminded suddenly that it hadn't been fed in a while, gave a loud rumble.

"See that?" Raif opened the door with a flourish. "I thought I saw a place on the way down here. The Sea Cucumber or something like that. Is it on a par with Rusty's?"

"No way. The Sea Chamber's for tourists, and anyway they require proper dress."

Raif eyed her appreciatively. Heather looked fine in her silky amber blouse and neat white slacks, but his cotton shirt and dungarees hardly qualified him for anybody's best-dressed list.

"So, where do we go?" he asked.

She considered. "Would you go for fried clams and soft-shell crab that cha-cha down your throat?"

"Sounds good to me."

Raif felt absurdly happy as he put the pickup in gear. Heather's cheeks were pink, her eyes sparkled with humor and she practically shone with health. The small bump on her head had all but disappeared. She was going to be fine, he reassured himself, and once again thought of what might have happened to her.

"If you won't junk that Mehitabel," he said abruptly, "at least have that mechanic—Eddy Simms, is it?—look at it. I know you're good at fixing machines," he added when she raised her eyebrows at him, "but it won't hurt to ask for a second opinion. I want you safe."

He really did care. Heather felt an unthinking happiness as she promised, "I'll definitely make sure Mehitabel's roadworthy before taking her out again."

"You'd better." Raif reached out and caught Heather's hand, gripping it tight. "I don't want anything to happen to my designer."

He smiled when he said that, and she intuited that work was far from his mind. Heather felt quite light-hearted when, still hand in hand, they arrived at the bank of a river.

"Okay," Raif said, "I'll bite. Where is it?"

He pulled into a gravel-lined parking lot and looked around. A stretch of river rippled before him. It was bordered on both sides by a tangle of palmettos, shrubs and reeds. Long-necked herons stood watch between oaks festooned with Spanish moss. A sleepy-looking pelican was perched on a pole stuck between a wooden jetty, a shack and several green, flat-bottomed motor boats.

"You're looking at it," Heather said.

She was pointing to the shack. She had to be kidding, Raif thought, or hallucinating. They'd driven all this way to go to a take-out stand?

Heather opened her door and got out. "At least look at the view," she said. "The Homosassa River is beautiful."

"I'm only humoring you because you're a sick woman." Raif swung his long legs out and let his boots crunch down on gravel. "Okay, the view is great. Now, let's go and—"

He stopped in midsentence as a breeze, wafting in from the direction of the shack, brought indescribable smells to tease his nose. Delicious smells. Fried-clam-and-crab smells. A wicked gleam lit Heather's eyes as she saw a rapt expression settle on Raif's face.

"Okay." She sighed. "If you really want to go, we'll find someplace else."

"As long as we're here," he began, then caught her eye and began to laugh. She laughed also, and he wrapped one arm around her shoulder, hugging her close against his side. "Let's go get those crabs."

Skipper Nate, a robust individual with apple-red cheeks and a tattoo of a blushing skunk on his forearm, greeted them from behind the counter of the shack. "What'll youse have?" he demanded in a thick Brooklyn accent. "Crabs are right out of the net, and I caught the shrimps myself this morning."

He got into an animated discussion about local fishing with Raif, and by the time their meal was ready they were on a first-name basis. "Tell youse what, Raif," Skipper Nate said confidentially, "this is the life. I worked my fingers right down to the knees for forty years. I froze my... earlobes off for forty years. Finally, my old lady and me decided enough was enough, broke the snow shovel in two, gave our itchy woollies to the Salvation Army and moved down here where it's warm."

Raif grinned. "You like being on vacation."

"Youse kidding?" Skipper Nate demanded indignantly. "I work harder here than I ever worked in my life. But here I enjoy it."

As he spoke he heaped crab, fried clams and broiled shrimp onto paper plates, filled others with a crisp garden salad and poured a subtle fruit punch into huge foam cups. Thus laden down, Raif and Heather emerged into the golden afternoon sunlight. There were wooden tables and benches on the sand some distance from the shanty, and stacks of neatly cut newspaper squares weighted down with a rock. "Napkins," Heather explained.

Crab eaten with a plastic fork had no business tasting like ambrosia, Raif thought. And the foam cups didn't detract from the drinks, either. He thought Heather would be pleased when he told her she'd made the right choice again, but she only said, "I knew you'd like it here."

She looked and sounded serious, and when she looked over the water, Raif saw that her eyes held that familiar shadowed look. The urge to draw her close and protect her was strong, but before he could make contact, she got to her feet and walked to the edge of the beach.

Sensing that she wanted to be left alone, Raif finished his meal and drink. When he finally strolled over to join her, she said, "Thank you."

"You're welcome. For what?"

"For giving me some space." In a low voice Heather added, "Nate's lucky that he and his wife are enjoying their lives together."

"Why does that make you sad?" he asked gently.

"The last time I came here, Sam and Maggie were with me. Now Maggie is all alone." Heather turned to look at Raif with troubled eyes. "It's not fair. They meant to go off on a trip together this year. They'd been saving their money. Now Sam's dead and the money's useless."

"Not useless," he pointed out. "Maggie's starting MM Pies with it. Sam would have wanted her to be independent. And it seems as though they were happy right here."

She was silent, and he searched his mind for something to say that would help. "While Nate and I were discussing fishing," he began at last, "I started thinking of my father. Dad was crazy about fishing, and we used to take a boat at Falmouth and go out for the whole day. Sometimes we'd catch something, sometimes not, but because we were together, it was precious time."

There was a new note in Raif's voice. Heather knew that he wasn't just talking about himself but about things that mattered deeply. She wasn't sure why, but she had the sense he'd never discussed these feelings with anyone else.

"Dad worked hard all his life but never made much money," Raif continued. "He tried his hand at many things, but nothing clicked until he bought a frozen-food company. He renamed it Raifoods after me for luck. It was small and had been mismanaged into the ground." He smiled reminiscently. "It became a family effort. My mother and I helped Dad until I went away to college. Then, while I was at B.U., Mom died, and life changed."

Heather put a hand on his arm. Covering her hand with his, Raif went on. "After my mother died, Dad put all his energy into Raifoods. He really loved that company, Heather, and it was his dream to see it become really successful. It was turning the corner when I graduated, but by then my father was already sick." Raif paused. "I guess what I'm trying to say is that life doesn't always turn out the way you want it to."

Raif's voice died away into a silence that lasted many minutes. After a while Heather said, "How I wish..." then went quiet again.

"What do you wish?"

His voice was soft, like an echo of the river. Heather felt those deep tones swirl through her, stirring emotions and sensations as she replied slowly, "Nothing original, I'm afraid. I just wish there was some kind of box into which I could put golden moments. Then when things weren't going right, I could spill out the brightness and relive good times." She paused to shake her head. "I don't know why I'm talking like this. Must be something in the punch."

She thought he would laugh and agree, but he only asked, "What would you put into your box?"

A thoughtful smile tugged the corners of her mouth. "Oh, a lot of stuff. Memories of my parents. The time I finally did a lube-oil-and-filter right and Sam gave me my Big S sweatshirt and said I'd earned it. One gorgeous, glorious day when I stood in the Catskills and looked up into a waterfall that was white with reflected sunlight. How about you?"

Maybe Heather was right about the punch, for Raif found himself thinking about this seriously. Perhaps the time he'd pitched a no-hitter back in Little League? That touchdown pass he'd caught in the fourth quarter with four seconds on the clock? Fishing with his father, surely, and the day Raifoods had come into its own. Good moments, all of them.

He looked at Heather standing there with the sun turning her hair to pale fire. "This afternoon," he told her.

Their eyes met. By wordless, mutual consent they leaned toward each other. "This is one memory I want to keep close to me," Raif whispered.

There was a series of loud splashing sounds behind them. Reluctantly turning, they saw Nate tossing fish into the water and pelicans diving after them. "Chow time," Nate shouted. "I feed them about this time every day, before the dinner crew comes in. Birds got to eat, too."

The putt-putt of a motor drowned out his voice, and a group of men, faces reddened from the sun, rode a flat-bottomed boat toward the jetty. "First of the fishermen coming in," Nate commented.

Soon this peaceful waterfront would become noisy and crowded and the delicately textured, precious moments that had been building between them would be lost. Raif looked at Heather and knew that she didn't want that to happen any more than he did.

"Do you rent out your boats?" he asked Nate.

"Sure. I usually charge by the hour, but seeing as it's late, I'll give youse a break if you want to take one out."

Raif queried Heather with a look, and she nodded. No words were needed to know that her thoughts paralleled his. They were in perfect sync. It was as though they'd stepped out of time and could ignore realities like Raifoods and New Mountain Farm and poor Mehitabel left nose to nose with a tree. Here there were only the river and the golden afternoon.

Happily she took her seat in the stern of one of the green boats and listened to Nate give Raif instructions and directions. "You go to your left and you'll come up to the wildlife sanctuary," he said. "Go right and you'll eventually end up in the gulf."

Heather opted for the gulf. "I haven't seen a real gulf sunset in a long time," she said as they glided away from the jetty. "How about you?"

"It's been a while since I watched any kind of sunset," he replied. "Usually, I'm at work till seven or eight."

He automatically glanced at his watch, and the reflexive movement seemed to jar the mood. Heather said, "I forgot how hard you work."

The subdued way she spoke took Raif unawares and made him look at her in surprise. "It's the nature of the beast, isn't it? I'll bet you put in long hours for P. and L."

"We did that."

She'd wrapped her arms around her knees as though for protection and there was a trace of unhappiness in her voice. Abruptly, Raif swore.

"I could kill him for hurting you."

She looked up to see that his green eyes were as hard as jade. "I'm talking about your ex-fiancé," he grated. "You were thinking about him just now, weren't you?"

Who'd mentioned Bill? He'd been the furthest thing from her mind. Heather was silent as Raif steered the boat under the bridge. Perhaps it was the shadow of the arch that darkened the boat, but somehow she sensed that the shadows went deeper. Raif's glancing at his watch had reminded her of realities she'd started to forget.

They were both silent as the motorboat chugged along between banks lined with palmetto and wild pepper trees and a few homes. The water was almost transparent, and Raif could see that the bottom was covered with waterweeds.

He mentioned this to Heather, who explained that the manatees fed on the weeds. "They're like huge walruses, right?" Raif asked.

She made an effort to recapture their earlier mood. "Now, if that isn't just like an ignorant Yankee. Haven't you ever seen a sea cow before?" He shook his head and she pointed to a sign that read Slow Zone—Manatee Feeding Ground. "You've got to reduce your speed."

Raif obeyed but said, "I hate to kick sand on your picnic, but at this rate it'll be sunrise before we get to the gulf."

There was a trace of impatience in his voice. "It can't be helped," she said. "Manatees come up from the gulf to find warm waters at this time of year, and they feed around here. They're so friendly and curious, they'll swim right up to a boat, and they're too slow to get out of the way of the motors."

Resignedly, Raif leaned back against the prow of the boat. "If we go any slower, we'll be standing still. Oh, well, I suppose that's in keeping with the rest of Mimosa."

She started to bristle, then saw the mischief in his eyes. "Now you're talking like a no-account, always-in-a-hurry Yankee," she countered energetically.

"Keep that up, and I'll call you Scarlett." Only that heroine didn't have that delicious sprinkle of freckles or a smile that could turn a man's heart inside out. Besides which, Raif recalled that Scarlett had been devious and selfish and hurtful while Heather was straightforward and funny and loyal. Raif found himself almost wishing that he was free to spend all his time here with her in the backwaters of Florida.

His thoughts were interrupted as Heather suddenly sat upright and exclaimed, "Raif, look there!"

The river seemed to have suddenly gone haywire. Huge puddles of mud oozed to the surface, destroying the lambent clarity of the water. Bits of chewed-up waterweed floated to the surface along with huge bubbles.

"Manatees," Heather said, adding excitedly, "They're feeding nearby. Kill the engine."

He obeyed, and they listened and watched as the muddy ooze spread, then eddied away on the river current. "Aw, rats," Heather groaned, "we missed them."

"No, we didn't. Look to four o'clock."

Two shadows, traveling slowly, were gliding through the water. One of the shadows was quite large, the other was smaller, sleeker.

Both shadows swam under the boat. Heather and Raif watched intently as they moved away leisurely. "Manatee and wife?" Raif wondered.

"No, mother and child. Manatees are rarely together except during mating season or when a mother is training her young."

"I guess they've got a modern outlook," Raif quipped, but talk of mating had brought George's morning remarks to mind. As Raif watched Heather leaning over the side of the boat, the responses of his body told him how wrong George had been.

"What's the joke?" Heather wanted to know when he laughed wryly at himself.

"Just something that George said this morning." Raif started the motor again, and very slowly they chugged through the water. "What happens if manatees get hurt?" he asked.

"They're taken to Sea World to recover. Later, they may go to the Homosassa Wildlife Sanctuary. It's a lovely little wildlife preserve where the birds come and go at will, and the gulf fish swim in and out as they please. It closes at six, I believe, but another time I'd be glad to show it to you. It's not far from here."

He started to reply that he'd like that and then remembered the time frame he was on. He didn't have time to sightsee, didn't have time to be out here on the river. By rights he should be back at George's right now, waiting for phone calls from Danny Hoaas and Ted Kovacheck. If they missed him they'd call back, of course, but was that what he wanted?

His thoughts went back to the troublesome Swiftee contract. His gut feeling of uneasiness came back stronger than ever, and he frowned. Through the years he'd learned to trust his instincts. Dammit, he needed to be in Boston so he could see for himself what was happening. Perhaps he should leave George to oversee things here and get back home.

Dimly, he realized that Heather was talking to him. "Is something wrong?" she was asking. "You've been sitting there staring into space for the last five minutes."

Reluctantly, Raif came to a decision. He'd turn the boat around now and head back to shore. Heather would understand. "It's getting late," he began.

She misunderstood him. "I know it's near sunset, but we're near the gulf."

Raif looked around him and realized that the scenery had changed. There were no more Manatee Feeding signs, and the river had turned a slate gray. The currents were growing stronger, too, and small waves rapped sharply at the sides of the boat. The houses along the banks of the river diminished in quantity and finally disappeared altogether.

"Heather," Raif said, "I really think we'd better head back. I've got to—"

He broke off as the boat came around a curve in the river and faced an incredible vista. The setting sun was poised inches from the distant horizon. Scattered clouds, colored in glory shades, hung breathless in the sky.

In order to get the best view, Heather began to move toward Raif. "Watch it," he warned as the boat rocked. "We don't want to watch the sunset *in* the water."

She didn't hear him, seemed hardly to register the fact that she'd fetched up against him so that her back rested against his knees. But even if she was unconscious of their closeness, he was all too aware. Thoughts of Raifoods faded rapidly as Heather's light weight pressed against him. Her nearness was tantalizing, and under the silky amber material, her breasts were rising and falling rapidly.

"It's so beautiful," she breathed.

Raif was looking at Heather, not the sunset. He watched how her eyes glowed, how the reflected colors warmed her peach-bloom cheeks and touched the corners of her definitely kissable mouth with gold. He felt positively light-headed with raw emotions he hadn't had since the days when he was a teenager obsessed with finding out all about love and sex, not necessarily in that order.

"I've seen a hundred sunsets and all of them are different," she was saying. "Oh, Raif, how can we think we're at all important compared to this?"

Somewhat dazedly, Raif realized that Heather was important to him. He cared about her.

"Look, Raif!"

He glanced up then, just in time to see the rim of the sun touch the water. "Looks as though it should sizzle," he commented.

Slowly, the sun sank out of sight and almost immediately, the sky began to dim. Heather sighed deeply and announced, "Show's over."

"Same time, same station tomorrow." Raif's arms tightened around her as he spoke, and for the first time Heather realized how close they were. Her back was wedged between his thighs, and his knees were on either side of her like the arms of an easy chair. But there was nothing easy in this proximity.

Her voice held a definitely ragged edge as she suggested, "Hadn't we better make tracks back to Nate's?"

Instead of starting the engine, he bent down to brush his lips against hers. The small kiss tasted of salt and fruit punch and the familiar Raif taste that burrowed deep into her body and worked itself into her heart.

With a strength of will she hadn't thought she possessed, Heather straightened and pushed herself free of his encircling arms.

"I mean it, Raif, we'd better get going. It's no joke being lost out on the river in the dark, and believe me, it gets dark awfully fast once the sun is gone."

She twisted her head to look up at him, but her words trailed away at the expression in his eyes. "Then let darkness fall," she heard him say before his mouth came down on hers.

Chapter Seven

Raif's cheek against hers was river-wind cool, but his mouth was warm. The strong clasp of his arms had become the perimeters of Heather's world, and the rocking of the boat was nothing compared with the giddy feelings that were spinning through her. Involuntarily her lips parted under Raif's, welcoming the deliberate invasion of his tongue.

Her mouth was sweet, the rose scent of her skin intoxicating. Time had become unimportant for Raif, and he took his time kissing Heather, relearning and savoring the shape of her lips and the satin inner linings of her mouth. Turning her in his arms so that she half faced him, he caressed her cool cheek, her warm throat, then dropped his hand to brush the fullness of her breast.

Intense pleasure seeped through Heather. Instinctively seeking more intimate caresses, she pressed herself against his questing hand and felt, through thin layers of cloth, the stroke of his fingers against her taut nipple.

One of his shirt buttons had come undone, and she wriggled her fingers through this opening. She explored his smooth skin and crisp chest hair and the velvet of flat male nipples that sprang erect at her touch.

Heather's fingers evoked a sweet madness in Raif. Still kissing her, he freed one hand so he could tug her blouse free of her slacks.

Against her fevered skin, his touch was cool. Heather tensed at the shock of that coolness, and he misunderstood. "Don't, sweetheart," he whispered. "Don't pull away from me."

Pull away? What she wanted was to get closer. Heather's body was quivering like a tightly stretched wire, and emotions and senses that she'd never felt before drained her of strength. She couldn't have pulled away now if she wanted to. She felt as weak as a day-old kitten.

"Just let it happen," Raif murmured against her ear.

Both of them knew exactly what would happen if this continued. And why not? Heather wondered. She hadn't been born yesterday. She wasn't living in the dark ages. She'd never felt like this, had never ignited so spontaneously to a touch or kiss. Raif had awakened primal needs that were rapidly going out of control.

Those needs practically screamed for satisfaction as Raif's lips caressed her earlobe, then took it lightly between his teeth, tasting and nibbling. *Let it happen,* he'd said, and Heather's insides agreed. They felt as if they were dissolving as Raif sucked softly at her earlobe.

Even her ears were erotic. They felt like silk and tasted like honey. Her soft curls caressed his face just as her hands were stroking his chest and back and arms. Raif let his hands do their own wandering as they smoothed over Heather's abdomen and roved upward until they found her breasts. When he worked his fingers under her bra, she shivered but made no protest.

Just then, something slapped hard against the side of the boat. It rocked violently, shocking them apart. "What in hell was that?" Raif exclaimed.

Woozily, Heather looked around her in the near darkness and saw a motorboat careening past them. As the wake of the bigger boat slapped their own craft around some more, Heather saw the skipper of the motorboat turn and wave.

He was grinning, and no wonder. Even in the twilight he couldn't have missed the fact that she and Raif were wrapped around each other like pretzels. Hastily, she disentangled herself.

"Even the big boats are heading back," she told Raif. "It's a warning."

He was having trouble thinking coherently. Every cell in his body was clamoring that he sweep her back into his arms and continue where they'd left off, and he had to forcibly remind himself that Heather was making sense. A flat-bottomed motorboat floating in the middle of the Homosassa river was no place for making love.

Reluctantly, Raif turned the boat around and began to head back. By now the sky had turned to shades of cobalt and purple, and the water was webbed with shadow. The moon hadn't yet risen and the riverbank was almost invisible. "You're right about one thing," he said. "It gets dark pretty fast here."

That wasn't the only thing that happened quickly, Heather thought. Cautiously, she made her way back to the opposite end of the boat.

"Are you sure we're going the right way?" she wondered.

"We'll be back at Nate's in fifteen minutes," Raif reassured her, then asked, "What was that sigh for?"

"Relief," she lied.

Maybe the bump on her head *had* cracked some vital reasoning mechanism, because a part of Heather was disappointed that they were heading for shore. This feebleminded part of her actually wanted to be lost out here on the dark water with Raif, to drift endlessly through sunrise and sunset, to be swept away by emotions too strong to control.

With an effort she shook her mind free of such idiocies and concentrated on what Raif was saying, something about it being a long time since he'd been out on the water.

He was thinking of his dad, of course. "I understand," Heather murmured.

Raif leaned back against the prow of the boat and tilted his face skyward. "It's difficult, but there's no alternative, is there? You have to do what you have to do.''

His deep voice was introspective, a little wistful. Heather had the almost irresistible urge to crawl across the boat and put comforting arms around him.

She said, ''It gets easier, really. When I lost my folks, I missed them like crazy. For the longest time, I couldn't even bear to walk past the park because we'd always picnicked there as a family.'' She paused. ''I know being on a boat won't ever be the same without your dad, but life does have to go on.''

''Without Dad?'' He sounded bewildered. ''I just meant that I've been too damned busy to see past the edge of my desk. Raifoods had an incredible growth year, and there wasn't much time to do anything besides work.''

He didn't sound unhappy about it, Heather noted. He sounded pleased with himself. Proud, in fact. His words and the tone in which they were said honed onto a raw spot in her mind.

While she'd been thinking feelings, he was talking business. While she'd been busy quelling the tumultuous responses of her body, his mind had been on his company. Apples and oranges. At times, she and Raif didn't even speak the same language.

As the thought touched her mind, Raif said, ''There's the first star of the evening. Make a wish, Heather.''

He was back on track with her again. His voice was warm and tender again. He was unpredictable and smart and loaded with sex appeal, and he was also going back to Boston as soon as his business with New

Mountain Farm was completed. Instead of looking at the star, Heather focused her attention on Raif.

He was sitting with his powerful body turned a little away from her, and she could sense that his attention was drifting again. Back to Boston probably, back to his beloved Raifoods. But he was watching her, too, for when a cool wind made her shiver he said instantly, "You're going to catch a chill. Come over here and let me keep you warm."

Heather wanted nothing in life more desperately than to bridge the short distance between them. It was incredible. It was illogical. It was also true that she could already taste his kiss. Her lips could almost savor the sweet salt flavor of his skin, and her fingers were tingling with the memory of how his chest hair had curled about the tips.

"I'm fine back here," she lied.

Raif knew she was lying because his own body was on fire. The distance that separated them didn't help—it just made him want her more.

I want you. Had he spoken, or had she been listening to the echo of her own thoughts? Almost desperately, Heather focused her attention on the white stars.

She was grateful when the boat grated against the jetty and one of Nate's helpers came running to moor the boat. It had become quite chilly, and Heather was shivering as they walked to the car. Raif's arm fitted around her shoulders as though it was the most natural action in the world, but when he drew her close to him, she muttered, "Let's not, okay?"

He didn't let her go. "Heather, in case you haven't noticed, I'm crazy about you."

She glanced up at him and instantly wished she hadn't. Illuminated by the spotlight above Skipper Nate's shack, Raif's eyes held so much desire she felt dazed by it.

Gulping hard, she tried for a light tone. "Know what ails you, Raif? Mimosa fever. It affects busy executives who don't have time to go fishing. Don't worry, it won't last. As soon as you get back to Boston, your sanity will return."

Instead of answering, he put his hands on each side of her, holding her between his hard warm body and the pickup. "Now cut that out," she tried to command, but her voice came out in a little whisper that didn't carry any kind of conviction.

"Heather, we're not kids." Raif leaned down until his forehead touched hers. "Is it so bad to want each other?"

As he spoke, a car pulled into the parking lot and several people got out. They shot curious looks in their direction and Raif groaned. "Let's go someplace else."

He smoothed back the curls from her forehead, his fingers gentle on the still-tender area of her bump. Gritting her teeth, Heather ignored the effect those stroking fingers had on her treacherous body. "You can take me back to Maggie's," she said.

But she was lying again. Shivers of desire were invading her as he continued to play with the tender spot on her forehead. Why, she wondered desperately, should his most casual touch evoke feelings that had to be illegal? "Raif, I want to go home," she repeated.

"Are you sure?"

She knew what he was asking. She also knew that if she repeated her request, he'd take her back to Maggie's without further argument. In fact, she didn't have to speak. All she had to do was nod, and yet she couldn't make that simple gesture. Taking advantage of her indecisive silence, Raif took her hand and lifted it to his cheek.

"I want to be with you. I want to make love with you, Heather."

The words thrummed in the air like music, and the tempo accelerated as he turned his head to bury his lips in the palm of her hand.

"I don't know," she said, and her voice was so troubled that Raif felt his heart clench into a frustrating knot of mingled passion and tenderness. He wanted to crush her to him and cover her face and body with kisses, yet at the same time he wanted to hold her gently, protectively. The tangle of confused emotions was so strong it was almost frightening, and he knew he had to do something physical or his control would shatter.

But when he bent to kiss her, her lips were cold. So were her nose and her cheeks and chin, and she was shivering. "My God, you're frozen," he exclaimed. "Get inside and let me start the heater. You'll warm up in a second."

Gratefully, Heather climbed into the pickup and felt the blast of its heater warm her bones. But though the physical chill was easily dispelled, the internal frost of uncertainty remained. Did she let her heart run away with her head? Did she let go of tomorrow and reach for today? Those questions had to be answered before things got out of hand.

Raif put an arm around her. "Better?" he asked.

Darn it, things were *already* out of hand. The people who wrote books about the joys of romance had it all wrong. Romance could be pure torture.

She didn't—couldn't—protest as Raif gathered her as close as the stick shift would allow. "What's troubling you, sweetheart? You know I care about you. You know I could never hurt you." His lips brushed hers in a light kiss. "I care about you."

And she cared about him. In that moment, nothing seemed to matter except the butterfly kisses that touched her mouth and chin and temples. Conscious of the treacherous tidal wave that was again building within her, Heather asked herself the big one. Did she or didn't she trust herself to start an affair with Raif?

Could she take what he offered—a moment of coming together, a night of passion with no strings attached—and be satisfied? When the night was over, could she return to her own life unchanged, still herself? If she could, she'd go for it, take the brass ring.

The problem was that she wasn't sure. Raif had confused her life as it was, and making love with him might change her forever.

Heather's voice was husky with the effort it took her to say, "I'm not into casual affairs, Raif. I know it's not very cool or modern, but that's the way I am. You'll be returning to Boston soon—"

He interrupted her. "What I feel for you isn't casual, believe me. And as for leaving, you know I'll be coming back to Mimosa often."

"You'd be coming here on business," she pointed out.

Why did she make that sound so wrong? Raif frowned as he protested, "We'll have time for each other, Heather. Dammit, I'll *make* time."

We'll have time for us soon, Heather, but right now I need to get this rendering done. You understand, don't you?

She understood every word he didn't say. The seething cauldron that was her body shut down. Heather could even predict what Raif was going to say next. He was about to suggest she return to Boston with him.

"What I'd really like," he was telling her, "is for you to come to Boston with me. We could get to know each other, take it as slowly as you like."

She couldn't forget—must not allow herself to forget—that though Raif's kisses turned her bones to jelly, though she felt happier with him than she'd ever been with anyone, the facts couldn't be altered. A leopard never changed his spots.

Quietly she said, "Let's not fool ourselves, Raif. You're going back to your world, and I'm going to stay right here in mine."

She definitely meant what she said, but Raif's trained ear caught an undertone of regret in her voice. The look that hardened in his eyes as he started the engine was one of determination. Heather Leigh was one stubborn woman, but he'd negotiated tougher deals before, and he was prepared to wait until her resistance wore down.

As they turned the corner onto Carver Street, Heather realized that the neighborhood was in complete darkness. Raif broke the silence that had fallen between them to remark, "I know that Mimosans roll up the streets after dark, but this is ridiculous. It's not even nine o'clock."

"Looks as if they've had a power failure," Heather agreed.

They drew up in front of Maggie's house and were greeted by the dim yellow eye of a flashlight. "That you, sugar?" Maggie called anxiously. "I didn't hear the old pickup banging, so I wasn't sure."

This was no time to discuss her minor accident. "It broke down again, so Raif brought me home." Heather alighted from the car and looked around her. "When did the lights go out?"

"They've been down for hours. I called the electric company, and they said that a tractor trailer knocked down a light pole on Main Street. They're working on it."

Maggie sounded mournful. When Heather asked what was the matter, she groaned, "The pies."

"I thought you weren't going to take any orders on Sunday, that you were going to take a rest." Maggie was silent. "Maggie, you promised."

"Sugar, I couldn't help it. Mr. Bergstrom, the owner of the Mandalay, called me personally—"

"That place? Why would they come to you? They've got their own pastry chef."

"Mr. Bergstrom said that the pastry chef had the flu and that the Rotarians were having some ritzy lunch at the Mandalay tomorrow. He read the letter we sent him— I guess we sent all the area restaurants a letter, sugar—and he felt this was a good time to try us out." Maggie paused for breath. "He gave MM Pies an order for twenty-five pies."

It would take hours to bake so many pies. Even if the lights returned, they were in trouble. "Could we bake them at someone else's house?" Heather asked. "Maybe Marie Turner's, or any of the ladies from your church group?"

"I thought of that, but Marie's power is out, too. It'd be a mess to transport all the ingredients, and besides, how could I spend the whole night in someone else's kitchen?" Maggie asked tearfully.

"Then you'll just have to phone Mr. Bergstrom and explain," Heather said, but Maggie wouldn't have it.

"It's the *Mandalay,* Heather. Besides, I can't get the reputation of being unreliable."

"Maggie's right." Raif had been so quiet Heather had almost forgotten about him standing there. "Do you have a phone book?" he queried. "Good. Then we can track down a generator."

"A what?" Maggie wondered.

Heather explained. "A generator produces electricity. But Raif, you'd never find a rental agency open at this time of night."

"Why don't we find out?" Raif ran up the steps to the house, gave Maggie's shoulder a comforting pat, then pulled out the phone book. As he began to work his way through the pages, he said, "A ten-kilowatt with two-hundred-and-twenty-volt capabilities is probably what we'd need."

Heather couldn't believe it. Within fifteen minutes, Raif had located a rental agency in Clearwater and ordered a generator, as well as a heavy-duty cable with a stove adapter. Heather was impressed. She'd never seen anyone so totally in command of a situation. Raif didn't doubt for an instant that everything would work out well, and his confidence was contagious. By the time he'd made arrangements for the generator to be delivered immediately, Maggie had lost her stricken look.

"Bet it's going to cost an arm and a leg." She sighed as Raif hung up the phone. "Oh, well, it can't be helped."

"Don't worry about costs, Maggie. This one is on Raifoods." Maggie began to object, but Raif took her hands in his. "I haven't thanked you properly for that fine dinner you gave me, Maggie Munroe. This is the least I can do for introducing me to your great pies. And, talking of pies, you'd better get ready to roll. The generator will be here soon."

Used to the ways of deliverymen, Heather wasn't too optimistic about that. She was astonished when, an hour later, a truck rumbled up with the generator in tow.

She went out with Raif and guided the driver to a flat place where the generator could be stationed, then ran back to the kitchen, attached the cable to the stove and snaked it through the kitchen window so that Raif could hook it onto the generator.

"You're pretty good as a gofer," Raif said when she'd joined him outside. "What else can you do?"

"Depends on what's needed. I carry a screwdriver in my pocket, blindfold roosters and slap pies together." As she watched Raif check the voltmeter, Heather wondered, "How come you know so much about generators?"

"On-the-job training, ma'am. I learned pretty quickly the first year Raifoods was in business. We had a hurricane, and the power shut down for three days. Since all our capital was stored in our freezers, we had to do something fast."

Heather groaned her sympathy. She was grateful that the tension that had simmered between them earlier had gone. This friendly talk was much safer, and besides, she enjoyed working with Raif. Strange, in all the months that she and Bill had been together at P. and L., she'd never really felt comfortable working with him. There'd always been an edge of rivalry between them, a subtle one-upmanship that had been generated by Bill. With Raif there was give-and-take and an exchange of ideas that made everything run harmoniously.

She glanced up at him and caught her breath. While she'd been absorbed in her thoughts, he'd been watching her, and the expression in those green eyes gave the lie to her earlier thought. The tension between them hadn't gone. Like a brush fire, it had just gone underground.

She swallowed hard and asked, "Are you ready to fire her up?"

Raif touched a switch, and a horrendous clatter ripped apart the quiet night air. Neighbors peered out of their doors and windows to see what was going on.

Maggie ran out onto the porch, but her objections died when her stove clicked into life. With a shout of "Hallelujah!" she plunged back into the kitchen.

As Heather started to follow, Raif asked, "Got another apron for me? Three pairs of hands are better than two."

He was as good as his word. As she busily chopped, peeled, grated and rolled out piecrust, Heather took time to bless Raif. His good nature and energy seemed boundless as he washed dishes and cooking utensils, beat egg whites till they formed stiff peaks, conveyed hot pies from the oven, swept the floor and washed down the counter.

Maggie said it all when, at three in the morning, they'd removed the last pie from the oven. "Raif, you're a gift from heaven. We couldn't have managed without you." She clasped her floury hands in front of her in a prayerful attitude. "Thank you from the bottom of my heart."

"I'm glad I was able to help. You've worked hard and I want you to succeed."

He spoke to Maggie, but his eyes were on Heather, and she knew that he'd done it as much for her as for Maggie.

"If I can make a suggestion," Raif continued, "you need a bigger oven—a modern one with a microwave. I hear that you're going to have a booth at the fair, and that's going to bring you more orders than this old stove can handle."

Heather raised her eyebrows. "You've changed your mind about our fair?"

Raif nodded. "George and I have decided to get a booth for New Mountain Farm."

She stared at him. "You're putting me on. I thought you felt Mimosa Fair was just for hicks."

"I'm smarter now. According to the stats, over a hundred thousand people came to the fair last year. You can't argue with numbers. Besides which, New Mountain Farm needs to show Mimosans that we support community affairs."

Maggie plopped down on a kitchen chair and surveyed her stove gloomily. "You're not fooling me, now. There really were that many folks at last year's fair?"

"Yes, ma'am. Exposure is what it's all about."

Heather listened carefully as Raif detailed his plans for his booth. The architects had put together a scale model of New Mountain Farm, he said, and these, together with Heather's drawings, should satisfy critics that the place wasn't going to be an eyesore.

For the second time today, Heather surveyed the man from Raifoods. His hands were white with flour, his apron decorated with meringue, and there were streaks of custard on his shirt. A leopard didn't change his spots, she thought, but suppose the leopard was really a pussycat?

The glow that lit his eyes was not a fanatical glow. The enthusiasm in his voice belonged to someone set on making a success of his business venture. Was anything wrong with success, for Pete's sake? Heather drew a deep breath, redolent with baking smells, then blinked as the lights flickered on.

They all cheered, and Raif said, "I'd better go and turn the generator off so the neighbors can get to sleep."

As he left the kitchen, Maggie stared after him with sparkling eyes. "Sugar," she announced, "I'm falling in love with that man."

Is that what's happening to me? Heather wondered.

Chapter Eight

The sky was bright blue, the sun was a true Mimosa yellow and the Grand Parade was winding down Main Street toward the park, which had been transformed into the fairgrounds. A troop of handsomely costumed Indians, cowboys and cowgirls trotted their palominos past cheering crowds and were followed by a convoy of old model cars and the Mimosa High School marching band.

Standing next to Heather, Raif watched the youngsters strut to Sousa. "They're not bad," he commented.

"One of these days they're going to make it to the Super Bowl, and they deserve it. They work like beavers."

Heather knew she'd acted like a beaver herself this past hectic week. The days had flown by in a blitz of preparing brochures and pies, and she might not have made it if Raif hadn't twice delivered much-needed eggs to Maggie's door.

He'd helped her even though he himself had his hands full. Besides overseeing the construction at New Mountain Farm, Raif had been meeting with poultry men interested in learning about Raifoods' newest venture. On Tuesday Raif had been in Tallahassee. He and George had flown up to North Carolina on Thursday. Yesterday, which was Friday and the eve of the fair, the two men had met with the president of a Georgia-based firm who'd flown down to Tampa to talk with them.

With all they had to do, Raif and Heather had missed each other all week. Twice she'd been at the printers when Raif brought the eggs. He'd been in Tallahassee when she took the finished drawings he'd commissioned to the farm, and she'd been out delivering pies when he phoned her to say he was delighted with how the sketches had come out.

Last night had been no different. While Heather had been running last-minute errands, Raif had come by Maggie's briefly to wish her luck and to tell Heather he'd pick her up in time to view the parade. She'd been up with the dawn, getting the MM Pies booth ship-shape. Now, standing beside Raif, she could relax and enjoy herself.

Raif seemed to be enjoying himself, too. He was laughing at the antics of some clowns who were tumbling and cartwheeling down the street and showering the crowd with candy. "Having a good time?" she queried.

"Haven't had so much fun in years." Lollipops flew their way and he fielded one and presented it to her. "Sweets to the sweet."

Raif knew he should be with George at their booth, but he hadn't been able to resist being with Heather. He'd missed her through the long week, which was why he was standing here and watching this parade. As he watched the sun put gold into Heather's hazel eyes, Raif wished the crowd would disappear so that they could be alone.

"It was nice of you to come by to see Maggie last night," she was saying.

"Fond as I am of Maggie, she wasn't the one I really wanted to see," Raif said. "I didn't get a chance to ask you before, but will you—"

He broke off as sirens shrilled nearby, and no less than ten fire engines came blasting and wailing down the street. Leaning closer, Heather shouted, "Mimosa's volunteer fire department."

"Are they expecting the Great Chicago Fire?"

"Most of the engines are on loan from surrounding communities. What were you going to ask me?"

Once more Raif attempted to ask his question, but his voice was drowned by the noise. "What?" Heather shouted.

"Will you go to the dance with me tonight?"

The sirens abruptly stopped just as Raif bellowed the question. People standing around them snickered, and a man in a Mickey Mouse hat winked at Raif.

"That's one way to ask a girl for a date."

Heather began to laugh, and Raif caught her hand and backed her away from the engines and the crowd.

"My ears are in shock," he complained. "So, will you go to the dance with me?"

"You don't know who you're dealing with. I'm the biggest klutz east of the Rockies when it comes to dancing anything but the polka." Heather pretended to sigh, but her eyes sparkled as she added, "But if you really want me stomping all over your feet—"

She was interrupted by cheers. "Now what?" Raif demanded.

"The mayor's limo just passed. Good old Jim Baxter is going to drive down to the fairgrounds and officially begin the festivities, so we'd better be getting to our booths."

Several streets had been cordoned off for pedestrians, and many people were walking the few blocks that would lead them to the park. Oblivious to the crowd, Raif and Heather strolled along hand in hand, bumping shoulders as they went.

"Were your meetings with the poultry barons successful?" she asked.

"They're impressed with our plans and with our product. As I told George, the timing on this is right." He paused, gave her hand a swing and added softly, "I missed you."

"I missed you, too." Then, as his eyes lit up, she added demurely. "We sure could have used an extra pair of hands in the kitchen."

But she'd missed Raif, all right. She'd missed his laughter and the feel of his hand holding hers. Above all she'd missed the electric something that always sparked between them. That spark was sometimes unnerving and could be downright disturbing, but it was an excitement she'd begun to crave.

"What's the dress code for the dance tonight?" Raif was asking.

"The rule is to 'come comfortable,'" she explained. "Avery always wears a suit and tie, but most everyone else dresses casually."

Raif had a sudden recollection of the black-tie affair that Raifoods had hosted for its employees and valued clients on New Year's Eve. It had been held at the Copley Plaza Hotel, and there had been at least five hundred guests. He'd started the evening with a headache that had steadily worsened in the swirl of booze and cigars and shop talk, and his date—Dorian something, a fashion model with great legs—had bored him with her chatter. She'd been beautiful but insipid compared to Heather. He'd been comparing every woman to Heather these days.

The way Raif was looking at her made Heather's cheeks warm. He looked as if he wanted to eat her with a spoon. The idle thought created images in her mind that caused her to give herself a sharp mental shake. "Looks like the whole of Florida's here," she commented.

As they reached the fairgrounds, Raif noted that there were several squad cars and uniformed police with walkie-talkies. The security personnel mingled with balloon and souvenir peddlers at the entrance. The grounds itself was lined with booths and concessions, and farther along were the antique cars, the pens for the 4-H displays and the space set aside for the egg-and-spoon race, the sack race and the three-legged hop, which would take place late on Sunday.

Open-air tables were manned by special-interest groups selling anything from crafts to hot dogs, and the booths were of various sizes and types. Some were elaborate and carefully decorated while others were small and functional. Maggie's was in between, a modest kiosk not far from the entrance. In front of the booth was an eye-catching wooden sign of a beaming woman in a chef's hat. *MM Pies* in big red, white and blue letters floated up in the steam issuing from the pie she was holding.

"Good work," Raif approved. "You've caught that rapt expression Maggie gets when she's baking."

They made their way to where Maggie was arranging small pieces of pie on a plate. "For people to taste," she explained. "They'll like what they taste and order, I hope."

"You'll have to beat them off with a stick." As Heather slipped around the back of the kiosk and donned a white apron, a booming voice rose in the near distance. "That's Jim doing his thing. We're officially open for business."

Guiltily, Raif realized George would be wondering where he was. "I'd better move on," he was beginning, when Maggie's groan stopped him.

"Oh, Lord. Isn't that Paula Portius?"

A tall, thin woman in a fashionable pants outfit was picking her way through the crowd. Her sunglasses, balanced on a long, aquiline nose, gave her the appearance of a dissatisfied bird of prey.

"Who's Paula Portius?" Raif asked.

"A local food columnist." Maggie's face had gone grim. "She writes a gourmet column for half a dozen suburban newspapers, and she's tougher than shoe leather. She never, ever, gives anyone a favorable review."

"Maybe she won't stop here," Heather said, but the tall, thin woman was making straight for MM Pies. "Don't worry, Maggie. She can't possibly find fault with your creations."

Raif watched the columnist nod regally to Maggie and Heather and pick up a sample piece of pie.

Maggie watched anxiously as the columnist chewed and swallowed. When she didn't say anything, Heather prodded, "Good, huh?"

Disdainfully, the woman flicked her fingers. "Well," she began, "I don't know how—"

"I myself don't know when I've tasted a better pie," Raif cut in smoothly. "Maggie Munroe's a baker in a thousand."

Heather watched as Raif turned his smile on Paula Portius. "Ms. Portius, isn't it? I'm Raiford Cornell." He paused while recognition and astonishment flickered in the columnist's eyes and then added, "I've been trying to lure Ms. Munroe away to Boston—we could use her magic touch at Raifoods—but she won't hear of it."

He had pitched his voice so that not only Paula but a dozen would-be customers clustering around Maggie's booth could hear. "That's Raiford Cornell, head of Raifoods," someone said in an awed voice. "I saw him having lunch with the mayor the other afternoon."

Raif turned the full charm of his smile on Paula Portius and said, "You're a connoisseur of food, so I'm sure you agree with me."

"Well, of course, Mr. Cornell." Paula Portius's strident voice had softened to a simper. "May I quote what you've just said in my column?"

"By all means." Heather, catching Raif's eye, saw him lower his eyelid fractionally. Aloud he said, "I have to be getting along, but I'll be back for more pie."

"You can have any pie you like," Heather said sincerely. "Anything at all. On the house."

"You say I can have anything I want?"

He smiled, and his green eyes rested on her lips. He was teasing and yet not teasing, but Heather didn't care. She was too happy.

"You bet," she said.

"I can't find the earrings that go with this dress," Maggie called from her bedroom. "Sugar, have you seen them?"

"Look behind the flowerpot on the sink," Heather advised.

Maggie appeared at the door of her bedroom dressed in a mauve print dress, white pumps and one large white earring. She clumped over to the kitchen sink, rooted behind a pot of African violets and sighed with relief. Then she paused and regarded Heather critically. "Aren't you dressed yet, sugar? Raif said he'd be here at seven, and it's five of."

Deliberately Heather whisked the iron over the silky material of her dress. "He and George were pretty busy today at the fair. He'll probably be late."

Maggie folded her arms across her bony chest. "I didn't raise you to be late for company, Heather Leigh."

"Why are you making such a fuss? It's just a dance," Heather began, then started as there was a whoosh of car wheels outside. "That's not him, is it?"

Maggie stumped to the window and peered outside. "Sure is."

"Oh, rats!" Throwing dignity to the winds, Heather picked up her dress and made a mad dash into her bedroom. Through the closed door she could hear the doorbell and Maggie exclaiming, "Now, Raif, don't you look handsome?"

When she'd last seen him, Raif had been shoulder deep in people. There'd been poultry men and egg men and people in the food business anxious to meet Raif and talk to him about Raifoods' new venture. She'd been sure he'd be late, but instead he was actually early.

"It's just a dance," Heather repeated, then caught a look at herself in her dresser mirror. With her tousled curls and that eager look in her eyes, she looked sixteen years old. "Stop being a ninny," she scolded her image, but the glow stayed with her. She was humming when, five minutes later, she walked into the living room and found Maggie and Raif sitting on the couch with their heads close together.

Heather thought they were comparing notes about the fair until she heard Maggie say, "That's the way my Heather is, Raif. Someday some very lucky man's going to appreciate—"

"What's this?" Heather interrupted.

They looked up at once, and Maggie said somewhat guiltily, "I was just bragging, sugar."

"About what?" But Maggie's reply was cut short as Raif got to his feet.

"You look lovely," he told her.

"You look pretty snazzy yourself." It was no lie. Dressed simply in well-fitting slacks and a sport shirt that had to bear a designer label, Raif looked both comfortable and elegant. A cashmere sweater, tossed negligently on the back of the couch, completed his fashionable image.

And he was holding out a florist's box, inside which was a single rose nestled in a spray of baby's breath. Its creamy white petals were tipped faintly with red that matched the red-and-white print dress she was wearing.

Her eyes shone as she looked from the flower to him. "It's perfect."

"So are you," he replied.

It wasn't gallantry. Raif had meant to present Heather with a spray of orchids or a dozen roses, and it was impulse that had made him select this one rose. Impulse and a poem he'd once read that had come back to tease his memory. "For the rose that is purest and dearest has a kiss of desire on the lips..." Heather *was* that white rose with the red blood of passion warming its petals. Looking down into her upturned face, Raif felt as if the world had suddenly stopped its turning. He had the nearly irresistible need to draw her closer and kiss her soft, smiling mouth.

"I think you should wear the rose in your hair." Maggie's brisk voice recalled him to reality. "Here, sugar, let me do it before you stab yourself. Doesn't she look a picture, Raif? Now, just let me get my sweater and we can leave."

Since three couldn't fit comfortably into the truck and George's car was laden with fishing tackle and assorted debris, Raif had settled for the best car that Mimosa Car Rental could offer. Maggie nodded approvingly as she settled herself into the back seat of the light blue luxury sedan and said, "Now, this is a lot more comfortable than my old wagon or that horrible old pickup Heather likes so much. Sugar, I sure do wish you'd junk that old heap."

"My thoughts exactly," Raif agreed.

"Nonsense," Heather protested. "Mehitabel has years of life in her."

"Now you sound exactly like Sam." To Raif, Maggie added, "If Sam had had his way, Heather would have been a mechanic and not a commercial artist. Know what, Raif? You two would have liked each other."

It was, Heather knew, Maggie's highest compliment. She swallowed the sudden knot in her throat and said, "Watch it, Raif. She's just buttering you up for the kill. Maggie, did you ask him if he'd endorse your pies on TV?"

"What's that?" Raif asked, and Maggie clicked her tongue.

"Oh, foot, I clean forgot. Thing is, I need a big favor." When he nodded, she went on somewhat nervously, "What you did for me today with that snooty Paula Portius was wonderful, and it got me thinking."

"What Maggie means," Heather explained, "is that several local cable stations will be coming to cover the fair tomorrow. We feel that this would be a great opportunity for MM Pies to get publicity, but we might not even be noticed unless the media people hear that Raiford Cornell approves of Maggie's pies."

Raif was silent for a moment, and Maggie rubbed her nose with a bony finger. "I know it's asking a lot. I'll understand if—"

"Hold it," Raif interrupted. "Listen, Maggie, just before I left George's, I had a call from Julia Thomas."

"You mean the news anchor from WKCZ? But that's a Tampa station," Heather exclaimed.

"Apparently she got wind of New Mountain Farm. She wants me to do a live interview about Raifoods and my reasons for choosing Mimosa as the site for my new venture." He paused. "What do you think, Maggie? Is MM Pies ready for a major-league network?"

Impulsively, Maggie leaned over the back seat and planted a loud kiss on Raif's cheek. "You're a dandy, that's what you are. But supposing Ms. Thomas doesn't want to hear about my old pies?"

"Let me worry about that. Just be at your booth, look charming, and be ready to answer questions at half past ten—that's the time Julia and I decided on.

But," Raif added mischievously, "the deal's off if you don't promise me a waltz."

Heather watched the older woman glow like a happy young girl. *Maggie's right,* she thought. *Sam would have liked Raif.*

But this sentiment was obviously not shared by Avery Lewis. Decked out in a rusty blue suit and a wide blue tie with red stripes, Avery was selling tickets to the dance at the long, covered table in the decorated and transformed high school gym. He gave Raif a sour look as he took his money.

"Sure was a lot of fuss about your farm at the fair today," he snorted. "I don't care, Cornell. I still don't think it's a good idea."

"Now, Avery, stop croaking like an old raven," Maggie scolded. "You said MM Pies would go under, and look at the profits I've already made."

Leaving the two arguing, Raif and Heather strolled into the gym. The Mimosa decorating committee had outdone itself, and the gym was bright with crepe-paper streamers, lights and yellow balloons. Branches of mimosa, both real and artificial, covered the walls, and a long, low table was already laden with food and punch.

"Looks a cut above the high school dances I used to go to," Raif was beginning, when the band struck up a spirited polka. He turned to Heather and bowed deeply. "Miz Leigh, ma'am, may I have this dance?"

Next minute, Heather was being whirled around the floor. The polka's one-two-three beat was simple enough to follow, and Raif was a strong leader. As she was danced about the gym, others drifted out onto the floor to join them.

"Who's in the band?" Raif wanted to know as they swirled past the bandstand. "They're pretty good."

"They're all volunteers. Doc Zermer's on the bass, and Norma Lighten's husband, Joe, plays the piano." Heather took a gulp of air. "Eddy Simms, from the garage, is on the clarinet."

"Too fast for you?" Raif grinned.

"No chance. I'm a Mimosa girl, remember? I could polka before I could walk. It's the sophisticated stuff I have trouble with. Waltzes, for instance."

As if on cue, the polka ended and a waltz began. "Now don't freeze up on me," Raif said. "Just let me guide you and your feet will do the rest."

She sighed. "That's all you know."

But she didn't want to leave the circle of his arms. That was the trouble, Heather thought. She didn't want to step away from him and end this moment. She caught a glimpse of Maggie dancing with Avery, and thought, *If she can, I can.*

"How come you look like you're sucking lemons?" Raif wanted to know.

"Don't you recognize intense concentration when you see it?" Heather winced as she trod on Raif's foot. "Uh, sorry."

She looked so serious and worried that Raif wanted to kiss the tense bow of her mouth. "Close your eyes and listen to the beat," he commanded.

Heather obediently closed her eyes and tried to listen. "One, two, three," she murmured. "*One,* two, three."

Raif whirled her onto the floor. "Keep counting," he ordered.

But her concentration flagged. He was holding her close against him and she could feel the hard press of his chest. The scent of his cologne invaded her senses until she forgot to count, forgot she was dancing, forgot everything except that he was holding her so closely. Suddenly she was aware that she was no longer treading on his feet.

"I'm waltzing," she exclaimed.

"By George, I think she's got it." Raif danced her around again, then slowed his steps as the waltz ended. "Nothing to it. You just needed the right partner."

"I guess." With an effort, she opened her eyes and looked about her. It seemed incredible that the gym was still full of laughing, talking people. Then she realized that some of those people were coming toward them.

One of them was Jim Baxter, the mayor. "Raif," Jim was shouting, "good to see you at our little gathering. I wanted to get over to see you today, but there were so many folks around your booth I couldn't get close."

Smiling his best politician's smile at Heather, Jim sidled in between her and Raif and began to pump his hand. As other men and women gathered around Raif, Heather stepped back and headed for the punchbowl on the long, cloth-covered table. As she was filling two plastic glasses, Avery Lewis came up beside her.

"Lost your partner, have you?" he commented.

"So have you." Heather looked around the gym. "Where did Maggie get to?"

Avery wasn't easily distracted. "Mr. Cornell has a lot of fans."

With an inner sigh, Heather noted that Avery's narrow face wore a deep scowl. Grooves of disapproval had been dug into each side of his mouth. "Why don't you approve of New Mountain Farm?" she asked.

Avery made a snorting noise through his nose and replied, "Once Mimosa lets industry in, there'll be no stopping things. But what does Cornell care? He doesn't live here."

"Jim Baxter sure does, and he seems to like the idea. Most people do, including Maggie."

Where was Maggie, anyway? The last she'd seen, she was chatting with some friends from her church group.

"All that glitters isn't gold, Heather," Avery was lecturing. "Cornell may be a smooth talker, but bear in mind that he'll go back to Boston and leave us with egg on our faces." He nudged Heather's arm, nearly spilling her punch. "Do you get it? Egg on our faces."

Heather gave Avery a cold look and began to walk away. The accountant followed. "I'm telling you people like Cornell don't think of anything but profit," he said. "The man's obsessed with making money, and he doesn't care what he does to Mimosa while he's getting it."

In a decidedly frosty voice Heather said, "Some folks just walked in. You'd better go collect their money, Avery."

She noted that George Montfort was among the latecomers. Decked out in a salmon-pink sport shirt and jaunty slacks, George looked like a satisfied whale. As he joined the group that surrounded Raif, Heather looked around her once again.

There was no sign of Maggie anywhere, and a nagging worry began to take hold. Perhaps in spite of her brave facade Maggie was missing Sam and feeling sad. Maybe she'd gone outside to be alone.

Setting down her glasses of punch, Heather stepped out of the gym door and into the cool darkness beyond. "Maggie?" she called softly.

There was no response from the darkness, but a moment later a dark shadow fell in beside her. "Thought you could escape, did you?" Raif asked.

"I wasn't escaping. I was looking for Maggie. And anyway, the last I saw of you, you were knee-deep in fans."

"I left George in charge. He's going to be Mr. New Mountain Farm, and he might as well learn how to deal with the public." Raif rocked back on his heels before adding, "As for Maggie, I spotted her going into the kitchen with some other ladies. They were having a deep discussion, so I wouldn't advise interrupting them for a while."

A samba had started back in the gym. Raif sent Heather a questioning look, but she shook her head. "The waltz is about all I can deal with for now."

"Then let's walk a bit and cool off." As they began to stroll away from the gym, Raif said, "Actually, George brought some interesting news. He just got off the phone with our prospective client in Georgia, who asked us to set up another meeting next week. He's anxious to negotiate terms of a contract with New Mountain Farm.''

"That's wonderful," Heather enthused, then paused at the quizzical look in Raif's eyes. ''Isn't it?''

''I'll tell you after the meeting. I'm in no hurry.'' Raif reached down and took Heather's hand, held it lightly clasped in his. ''But I didn't come out here to talk business. I came to be with you.''

Her heart gave a little bump. ''Not according to good old Avery. You're a money-mad Yankee who's out to exploit and ruin Mimosa—or so he thinks.''

''And do you know what *I'm* thinking right now?''

They stopped in the shade of a tall, fronded palm. It rustled softly in the breeze as Raif took Heather's other hand and drew her slowly toward him. ''That I'm a terrible dancer?'' she tried to joke.

''Guess again.'' But before she could, his mouth had found hers. Almost instinctively her eyes closed and her head tipped back.

Their lips came together as though obeying some unseen magnetic force. As Raif's arms closed around her, Heather knew she'd been wanting his kiss, waiting for it all day, all week. Now she was lost in sensations evoked by the erotic taste of his mouth and the way his tongue nudged her lips until they parted under his. The tender-rough feel of his cheek against hers and the hard press of his muscular body holding her close—she'd dreamed about this.

But Raif was no dream. His hands were very real as they roved over her back, down the ridges of her spine to cup her buttocks and lift her up to him, against him. She could feel the urgency of his want as he whis-

pered her name and scattered small kisses across her
face, her cheek, her chin, her throat at the cleavage of
her dress. The warmth of his lips stroking her bare
skin awoke responses that were nothing short of primal.

Heather moaned softly as Raif's open mouth slid
down to trace the inner curve of her breast. His hunger and his virile heat seemed to penetrate dulling layers of cloth and suffuse her waiting flesh with warmth.

Her knees had gone so weak it was a blessing there
was a bench beneath the palm. Still fused together,
they sank down on it, and Raif whispered, "Heather,
don't you think we've waited long enough?"

Too long, she thought. *Much too long.*

"We could leave now and be together." Controlled
passion throbbed in Raif's voice, and Heather felt
dizzy as that passion ignited, blazed through her.

"What about Maggie?" she whispered.

It was surrender, and they both knew it. Raif's voice
had a husky edge as he said, "George will take her
home. I'll plead business, you'll say you're tired.
That's all anyone need know."

Raif sure didn't know Mimosa, Heather thought,
but she didn't care if people gossiped about her. She
didn't care about anything. Her body was afire with
need for Raif, a need that had been kindled since their
first meeting. She wanted him to make love to her tonight, now, this moment. She wanted him more than
she'd ever wanted anyone or anything in her life.

It all came down to a question of trust. She either
cared enough about Raif to trust him or she didn't. It
was that simple. And as Heather looked up into Raif's

moon-silvered eyes she knew her answer. Raif's eyes were full not only of passion but of tenderness. She could trust a man with eyes like that.

Deliberately, she reached a hand to caress his cheek. He kissed the palm of her hand, and she smiled at him with her heart in her eyes.

She didn't say anything and she didn't have to. Raif could feel her thoughts by the way the tension left her slender body, by the way her lips curved into a tremulous smile. *Yes,* he thought. Finally Heather was willing to live for tonight and let tomorrow take care of itself.

She trusted him. Raif felt an ache in his gut that had nothing to do with the desire that was searing through him. This was a different heat, an urgency rooted in the need to protect Heather as well as to possess her.

Earlier along, he'd noted a motel along the way, but it was too close to town and someone might recognize Heather or the rented car. Along Route 19 would be better. Rising, Raif drew her up into his arms, then slid his hands down so that they locked behind the small of her back. As her softness seemed to meld with his hard body, Raif's ready imagination threw out fevered images of another kind of melding.

"Let's go," he said just as there was the sound of muted laughter behind them. A man and a woman, arms wrapped around each other, hurried past them into the shadows.

"Oh, Lord," Heather murmured.

"They didn't see us," he reassured her, but she was shaking her head.

"I wasn't worried about them seeing us. That was Link Benson together with Amelia Kerr. She's Eddy Simms's fiancé. When Eddy finds out, there's going to be big trouble."

She'd said "when" and not "if." As the rationale for her choice of words registered in Raif's passion-fogged brain, he suddenly realized what Heather had known all along. It wasn't possible to keep a secret in a place like Mimosa. Back there, the gym was jam-packed with busybodies who would gladly tell Eddy what his girl had been up to—or what Heather Leigh was doing with Raif Cornell.

That was what living in a small town was like—everyone knew everyone's business. If he took Heather away now, someone with sharp eyes and a nasty tongue would start the gossip. There'd be whispers and sly looks and innuendo—and pain for Heather. Though he didn't give a rap about what Mimosans thought or said about him, Heather was different.

This was her home, her folk, and she cared about them. With a long breath that was almost a sigh, Raif held Heather close to him. For a long, regretful moment, he drew in her scent of sunshine and roses, then dropped his arms from around her and said, "We'd better be getting back."

Getting back?

Ignoring her look of bewilderment, he slid an arm through hers and began walking her back to the gym. "Back to the dance before Avery sends out a search party."

Raif's voice was husky in spite of his efforts to keep it casual. He'd just realized how much he'd come to care about Heather. It was almost as if he were in love with the woman.

Chapter Nine

Heather stood by her bedroom window, leaned her elbows on the sill and cupped her chin in her hands. Sleep was a million miles away, and she'd stopped trying for it.

She'd accepted the fact that, given the electricity that had simmered between Raif and herself since they first met, all that had happened tonight had been pretty much inevitable. It was what *hadn't* happened that was keeping her awake.

She was still having trouble with her body, which continued to smolder from the igniting touch of Raif's hands. She could taste Raif's mouth, and the remembered brush of his fingers against her breast brought images that would have made a censor blush.

The intensity of her feelings was almost scary, and by the time she tried to halt the memories, the damage had been done. Heather's skin tingled as though stroked by electricity, her breasts ached, her lower limbs seethed with a honeyed heat. If Eddy Simms's two-timing finacée hadn't come by when she had, she'd have gone anywhere with Raif, gone without reservation or thought for the future.

Admit it, Heather, you've fallen in love. But love was commitment, wasn't it? It was what her parents had had, what Sam and Maggie had shared, it was about planning to grow old together.

And she'd been wrong about love before. Heather tried to think straight. She remembered that just before she and Bill had split up, she'd been in such a state she'd actually sat down and written out a balance sheet of the pros and cons of their relationship. It had helped her clear her mind.

Okay, she thought, *here goes.* On one hand was the fact that she felt good when she was with Raif. He was dependable and funny and made her feel as special as any woman could and still walk the ground.

Heather had a swift mental image of herself dressed as Justice with a set of scales hanging from her hand. Those scales, which had been clearly tipped in the pro direction, suddenly dipped down as she thought of Raif's devotion to his work. They started to tip down farther as she remembered his admission that he hadn't seen past the edge of his desk for a whole year. The man worked around the clock and the week, for Pete's sake. He grew impatient with delay. His brain was like a Wall Street ticker tape, always looking for new business strategies and ventures and angles. And to top it all off, Raif was leaving for Boston soon.

How could there be a relationship under such conditions? It was impossible. But just when the scales

were sinking under the weight of her objections,
Heather thought of tonight. Tonight, when her own
reasoning processes had deserted her, Raif had acted
to protect her reputation.

Instantly the scales balanced out in Heather's mind.
She could *trust* Raif.

New Mountain Farm would bring Raif frequently
to Mimosa, and since Maggie was making a success of
her business, she, Heather, could start thinking of her
own future again. Suddenly she felt happy and light-
hearted, as though luminous moonbeams were filter-
ing into her and making her as light as air. Perhaps her
future might include going to Boston. Raif had said
there'd be no strings attached, and she believed him.

Working with Raif would be exciting. Being with
him would be exhilarating. And for the rest... "Go for
it," she told herself. "Go with the flow and see what
happens."

Heather felt like a kid on Christmas Eve, counting
the moments till tomorrow. She couldn't wait to be
with Raif again.

Raif awoke to find himself on his side with his arm
curved blissfully around his pillow. His dream had
been so vivid that he could swear that the cotton fabric held Heather's scent.

For a moment, he considered going back to sleep
and recapturing that dream, and then he looked at the
clock. "Good Lord," he groaned. "Nine o'clock."

He'd forgotten to set his alarm for six-thirty. He'd
wanted to do some jogging. Physical activity always
sharpened his mind, and he needed to think through
his interview with Julia Thomas. He'd intended to jot

down some notes so he could brief Julia on the points he wanted to discuss during their interview. Since he was certain the interview would be cut before being aired, he wanted everything he said to pack a publicity wallop.

Raif swung his long legs out of bed and hit the floor on the move. When he reached the bathroom, he found George had taped a note on the mirror. "See you at the booth, old son," George had scrawled.

Raif turned on the shower and yelped as a jet of icy water hit him. He needed the proverbial cold shower this morning, could have used the same treatment last night. His thoughts as he tossed and turned in the moonlight had been unbelievably erotic, and when he'd finally dozed off, his dreams had gone totally out of control.

Awake or asleep he'd been with Heather, holding her, kissing her, registering the firm, sweet swell of her breast under his hand and the taste of her lips and the rose-and-sunlight scent of her skin. Raif grinned wryly. The cold shower wasn't helping, and his newly awakened body was demanding to know why he hadn't fulfilled his fantasies last night.

The answer to that one was pretty obvious. Not being a totally selfish clod, he'd realized how much Heather had come to trust him. And that meant that he couldn't do anything that would hurt her or set her up for future unhappiness.

Was he falling in love with her? Raif wondered. Last night, the question had come out of left field and hit him like a two-by-four. Now it had taken root in his mind, but he still didn't have the answer. He'd thought himself in love before, but none of the women he'd been interested in had come close to Heather.

Heather was multifaceted. She was a capable woman who could work beside him on anything from machinery to art. She was independent and loyal and funny, and her presence could light up a room. And he couldn't seem to keep his hands off her.

In the relatively short while he'd known her, Heather had become incredibly important to him. On her part, she seemed willing to take the next step in their relationship. But her willingness to embark on an affair with him created some difficulties. Raif had to admit that any love affair begun now would have to be largely a long-distance romance fed by phone calls and ignited by infrequent meetings.

No, Raif thought, *no way. I want her with me.*

That meant he had to persuade her to come to Boston with him. From what Maggie had told him last night, Heather's former fiancé had been a fool who had had time for everything but Heather, and she was probably afraid that if she made the move to Boston, she could end up ignored. If he could prove to her that this wouldn't be the case, she might agree to take the step that would let their relationship grow.

But grow into what? That was the kicker. Raif had been attempting to grapple with that question last night when he fell asleep, and it was still giving him trouble. Heather was important to him, yes, but how far was he prepared to go? He wasn't at a stage in his life—dammit, he *didn't* have the time—to settle for a total commitment. Raifoods had become ready not only to expand in New Jersey but also to branch into the southern states. Raifoods needed him. It needed his time and his expertise and his energy at this critical stage of its growth.

But then there was Heather. He couldn't be casual about her; he couldn't even be moderately committed. She was the kind of woman who would commit all of herself to a relationship.

Raif frowned. He realized that she'd already started to change his way of thinking and of living. The fact that he'd stayed on in Mimosa was twenty percent due to New Mountain Farm and eighty percent because of Heather.

Perhaps what he needed was to return to Boston. Distance provided perspective, and he might be able to make a better decision overall if he had time to think things through without Heather's distracting presence.

Raif was interrupted in midthought by the shrilling phone. Switching off the shower, he wrapped a towel around his lean middle and went to the phone by his bedside. Expecting to hear George demand where the hell he was, he was startled to hear a familiar, rasping voice ask, "Did I disturb you, boss?"

Immediately, he smelled trouble. "What's gone wrong with the Swiftee deal?" Raif demanded.

Ted Kovacheck sounded concerned but not worried. "One of their vice presidents—Jerry Hoyt—has left the firm. His replacement, Will Connor, wants to meet with our negotiating team before signing the contract." Ted paused before adding, "We're on top of things here, Raif, but I knew you'd want to know."

Listening, Raif damned himself for not being in Boston. "I'm flying back to take charge of this personally," he said.

"There's really no need," Ted argued. "Danny and I have talked it over, and our gut feeling is that Connor isn't really objecting to our contract. He's just throwing his weight around. We've arranged to meet so that we can—"

Raif interrupted at this point. "I can't afford any more delays, Ted. Set up a meeting with the Swiftee people first thing tomorrow morning. You and Danny meet me at Logan tonight, and both of you be ready to fly with me to Newark tomorrow." As Ted rasped assent, Raif added crisply, "Now, tell me everything you know about Connor. I want to know who I'm dealing with and what problems we can expect."

"If he doesn't get here soon, we'll have big problems," George said.

"It's not ten-thirty yet," Heather said. "He'll be here."

George's usually cheerful and optimistic face was furrowed with anxiety. "This isn't like Raiford. He's usually punctual to the point of being compulsive."

"Maybe he overslept." But Heather didn't believe her own words. Sleep hadn't been in her vocabulary last night, and she couldn't believe that Raif had slept, either.

She glanced over her shoulder at Maggie, who was nervously arranging and rearranging her pies. Maggie had been beside herself this morning, trying on every dress she had and attempting to coax her hair into a fashionable upsweep. She'd fussed with makeup and jewelry until she'd finally worn herself out. "Sugar," she'd mourned, "I'm as plain as an old shoe. I hope the TV people bring their makeup artists. I'm going to need all the help I can get."

To Maggie, this TV appearance was one of the high points of her life. Raif understood that. So where *was* he? He should have been here an hour ago.

Maybe his car had broken down, Heather thought, but the explanation wouldn't wash. Even if that had happened, Raif could have called a cab or hitched a ride. Mimosa was the kind of place where people always stopped to help out someone who was in trouble.

"George," Heather faltered, "do you think that he...that he's been in an accident?"

Apparently this possibility had occurred to George. "I wouldn't be surprised," he gloomed. "These snowbirds coming from New York drive like maniacs."

Raif involved in an accident. Raif lying in a hospital. Raif—God forbid—in the morgue. As images passed in horrible sequence through Heather's mind, there was a commotion in the near distance, and a van with WKCZ-TV on its side drove slowly up to the fairgrounds. "Oh, my stars," Maggie moaned. "Here they are."

With a sense of foreboding, Heather watched security police wave the TV van into the fairgrounds. It parked near the first cluster of booths, and a tall, dark-headed young woman in a stylish denim jacket and skirt emerged.

Heather recognized the prominent cheekbones and keen blue eyes of the well-known news anchor, Julia Thomas. As Julia's light, sound and camera crew appeared from the van, George rumbled, "I'll have to wing it. Heather, come with me."

As she hurried to keep pace with George, Heather scanned the fair for Raif. He was nowhere in sight.

"Let me do the talking," George warned.

Heather listened as George introduced himself and added that his partner was on his way to the fair. "Miss Leigh is our publicity coordinator. Until Raiford arrives we can show you what New Mountain Farm is all about."

Julia Thomas frowned a little. "Can you tell me why Mr. Cornell has been delayed?" she asked.

"All I can say right now is that there's been considerable interest in Raifoods' newest venture." Pausing to let this sink in, George continued to stretch the truth. "Preliminary negotiations are delicate, Ms. Thomas. My partner won't let anyone else handle matters at this stage. Of course it's his hands-on policy that has made Raifoods a household word."

Even in her anxiety, Heather had to appreciate George's style. His voice boomed like a brass gong and his large body fairly quivered with sincerity. Julia Thomas looked regretful as she glanced at her watch. "I understand what you're saying, but we're on a tight schedule and can't afford to wait for Mr. Cornell to arrive."

"Perhaps you could cover the fair first," George suggested. "I'm sure you know that local color as a backdrop can be most effective."

Heather thought it time to add a suggestion of her own. "Perhaps you could begin your coverage of the fair with that booth," she said. "Mr. Cornell plans to talk about MM Pies during his interview with you."

"I don't know anything about that," Julia Thomas said, but Heather wasn't about to give in without a fight.

"As Mr. Cornell's publicity coordinator," she said firmly, "I know that MM Pies is of great interest to him."

Right on cue Maggie called, "Here, Miss Thomas. Try some of my Key Lime Fluff."

She smiled invitingly, but Julia Thomas shook her head. "Sorry, I'm on a diet. Besides, we've got to get moving. Mr. Montfort, let's go to your booth and shoot some stills. We can get some footage of the fair on the way."

"What about you young people?" Maggie shoved her plate of samples toward the crew, who each took a piece before they hurried after Julia Thomas and George.

With a despairing look at Maggie, Heather followed also. She hoped that she would be able to convince Julia Thomas to give some mention to Maggie's business, but she didn't get the chance. Beyond shooting some stills of the New Mountain Farm prototype and Heather's drawings, the TV anchor seemed interested only in Raifoods and its expansion into the south.

There still was no sign of Raif. Heather's heart sank as the minutes marched inexorably past, and finally, at fifteen minutes past eleven, WKCZ packed it in. As the television van slowly drove out of the fairgrounds, Heather returned to Maggie's booth.

The booth was doing a brisk business, but Maggie looked so forlorn that Heather couldn't meet her eye. "I'm sorry," she said, sighing.

"You gave it a durn good try, sugar." Maggie made a heroic attempt to sound cheerful but then added, "What worries me is where Raif is. I just pray that nothing awful's happened to him."

Heather felt sick to her stomach. The fear in Maggie's eyes completely matched her own. Suddenly she felt as though she were young and frightened, sobbing at the hospital after her parents' death.

"I'm going to try the farm," she said.

Hurrying to the public phone that stood near the entrance to the fair, Heather dialed the farm's number. She could hear her heart pounding as the dial tone whirred and clicked and then went into George's recorded voice. "You have reached New Mountain Farm. If you'll leave your name and number—"

Heather hung up, dropped another quarter in the coin slot and dialed the police. The desk sergeant told her that there had been no report of accidents on the highway. Then before she could feel relieved he added, "But then again your friend might have gotten into a minor accident or broken down someplace or suffered a heart attack or stroke by the roadside. Things like that do happen."

The sick churning in Heather's stomach intensified. She didn't know what to do next. *Raif, what's happened to you?* she wondered.

"Heather, over here!"

She almost stopped breathing for a moment as she recognized the voice. Her heart slammed into renewed life as she saw Raif striding toward her. She wanted to run to him, but her legs had gone weak, and she was rooted to the spot.

"Are you all right?" she stammered.

Raif couldn't hear what she was saying. "I know I'm late," he called. "Where's Julia Thomas?"

"They've come and gone," Heather explained.

"I hope George handled things. If they shot some stills of your drawings and the scale model, it's not a total loss."

Heather took a gulp of air and said, "Never mind about that. We've all been terribly worried about you. Raif, you're more than two hours late. What happened?"

There was a grim look in his eyes. "A phone call happened."

He wasn't making much sense, Heather thought, but at least he was here, he was safe and he looked uninjured. There had been a moment when she'd really believed that something awful had happened to Raif, and in that moment she'd felt as though her own life had been suddenly cut short.

She wanted to tell him this, but he was already striding off in the direction of his booth. She hurried after him. He looked preoccupied and impatient and was definitely acting odd. Heather remembered that he'd mentioned something about a phone call and asked, "Was your call an emergency?"

This time, the anxiety in her voice got through to him. "I'm sorry, Heather," he said. "It's just that the roof fell in on me this morning. It's my fault. I had a feeling about the Swiftee deal and should have been more on the ball."

She blinked. "The what?"

"A merger I thought was concluded," he replied shortly.

He hadn't been in an accident and there hadn't been any emergency. Raif's *work* was what had detained him.

"If I'd been in Boston, I could have pushed the contract through," Raif was saying. "I should have my head examined for not getting involved personally long before this. It wasn't Ted's or Danny's fault—it was mine."

"So now you'll handle things, naturally."

Immersed as he was in his problems, Raif didn't note the bitter tone in Heather's voice. "I'll explain later," he told her. "Right now I need to talk to George."

As she listened to Raif's crisp voice, Heather's mind did a back flip through time. The words were familiar. The routine of checking the watch and frowning was right on cue. And she'd seen that preoccupied look a hundred times before.

And she'd *trusted* him. She'd thought him dependable and kind. She'd cared so much about him that when she'd realized he might be hurt, her life had actually seemed to cave in.

"You idiot," she whispered.

He glanced sideways at her. "What's that?"

"I was talking to myself." Heather dragged a deep breath into her lungs, and his familiar scent brought memories that pushed her blood pressure up several notches. "You should have your head examined, you say? Well, that makes two of us. I knew whom I was dealing with and what I was getting into. But did I listen to reason? Not this fathead."

Raif hardly heard her. Looking about him, he'd seen that though WKCZ-TV had left the fairgrounds, the local cable channels were in the area. Perhaps he could still get New Mountain Farm—and Maggie—some media attention. "Look," he told Heather, "whatever it is that's bothering you, we'll talk about it later."

Be a good girl, Heather. Wait till I've finished doing what's really important.

A white-hot point of pain began to pulse in Heather's brain. She stopped dead in her tracks and announced, "We'll talk about it right *now*."

He stopped also. "What's got into you?" he demanded.

"Did it ever occur to you that Maggie counted on you?" she cried. "She couldn't sleep last night worrying about the TV spot. She got up at dawn to try on all the clothes in her closet. It was 'Raif this,' and 'Raif that,' all the way. Being interviewed by Julia Thomas mattered to her. But one stupid call from Boston, and you forgot that Maggie even existed."

As he listened, Raif felt a rush of anger. He didn't need this after a trying morning.

After a long conversation with Ted, he'd spoken with Danny, then phoned Swiftee's president. After that he'd booked a night flight out of Tampa. He could have taken an earlier flight and had a much-needed briefing with Ted and his negotiating team this afternoon, but instead he'd come to this fair.

"I can't believe it," Raif muttered.

He'd opted to let the Swiftee merger sit on its thumbs until tomorrow morning in order to keep his promise to Maggie, and here was Heather shouting that he was some kind of traitor.

"Lower your voice!" Raif snapped. "I'll make it up to Maggie."

"Oh, right," she came back. "You're going to drive after WKCZ and drag Julia Thomas back here by her microphone."

"You can be as childish as you want later—"

"Childish!"

"But right now, I have to talk to George. And then I intend to talk up MM Pies on the local cable network. That is if they all haven't left while you were throwing your tantrum."

Restraining an impulse to kick him in the shins, Heather drew herself to her full, quivering height. "Let me see if I understand you correctly. I'm childish because I happen to care about people and their feelings. You, on the other hand, have other priorities."

"Have I?"

His voice had gone deadly calm, and his controlled fury only served to stoke her rage. Heather's control snapped like a stretched wire. Oblivious of the people who were turning around to look at them, she yelled, "All you care about is your precious Raifoods. You breathe and eat your work and you don't care what happens to the people around you. You forget they even exist."

Anger snarled about them like electricity gone haywire. Fury and hurt blazed at her out of Raif's green eyes. But Heather was in too much pain herself to see his conflicting emotions.

"Have you finished?" Raif grated.

"Yes. I have nothing more to say to you, *Mr.* Cornell."

And he'd thought he knew Heather. This wasp-tongued vixen that confronted him was a total stranger. Raif seethed as he remembered how he'd wanted to protect her. From the way she was carrying on, he was the one who needed protection.

He'd been out of his mind, Raif knew. Temporary insanity, a touch of the sun, whatever it was, he was over it, thank God. And once back where he belonged, he'd be able to forget just how close he'd come to making a fool of himself over this hazel-eyed witch.

Biting off each word as if he hated it, he snarled, "You've made your point. Now get out of my way and let me get to work."

Let me get to work.

As the too-familiar words filtered into her brain, the pain inside Heather's head became a supernova. "You can go straight to hell," she shouted.

They glared at each other for a long moment. When he spoke, Raif's clipped voice was like ice. "Thanks for the advice," he said, "but if it's all the same to you, I'm going back to Boston."

Chapter Ten

Eddy Simms ran a critical eye over Mehitabel and commented, "This poor old heap sure did need maintenance."

Assenting, Heather wiped her hands on her grease-stained overalls. "Thanks for the use of your lift, Eddy."

The mechanic nodded but didn't smile. Smitty, the mechanic who'd worked for Sam and who was now Eddy's right-hand man, had said Eddy hadn't cracked a smile since he and Amelia broke up.

"You done a LOF on her?" Eddy was asking.

A lube, oil and filter had been the first thing on Heather's list. She'd also done a tune-up, tightened the radiator hose and checked Mehitabel's brakes. "Brakes are okay, the tires are fair, but the front shocks are getting rather soft," she commented. "I'll get to them next week. Right now, though, I have to finish with this tie-rod end."

Eddy watched approvingly as Heather tightened the nut and put in the cotter pin. "If you weren't so gosh-darn busy with all that advertising stuff you do, I'd offer you a job. Sam would be proud of you."

As she smiled her thanks, Heather wondered if that was why she'd been working so hard to get Mehitabel roadworthy. The pickup had been sitting in the Big S since being towed in from New Mountain Farm. Eddy would have gotten around to fixing her this week, but Heather had opted to do the repairs herself. Though her "advertising stuff" kept her busy these days, working on Mehitabel seemed to bring her closer to gentle, patient Sam and gave her a measure of peace.

But today there was no peace. Today Eddy wanted to talk. "Hear that Maggie's doing good," he commented. "Avery says that she signed a contract with George Montfort and that she's going to get all the eggs she needs at a good price." Heather nodded. "Heard she hired Thelma Carruthers and Lil Shea to help her bake, too. But she made a mistake picking Bernard Jakes to deliver her pies. Boy's as slow as molasses in January. Avery says as how it took Bernard half an hour to drive his car from Maggie's to the Proud Pelican."

"Avery should get a job at the *Mimosa Herald*," Heather commented. "So Bernie's careful. So what?"

"Maggie's going to need somebody with more pepper in him, that's what. She's gotten awful busy since the cable TV channel carried those interviews with her." Eddy nodded sagely. "Even Avery had to allow as Raif Cornell did a handsome thing, endorsing MM

Pies on cable like he did. What do you hear from Raif, Heather?''

Ignoring the question, Heather tightened the sleeve that held the tie-rod end. "That should do it. I think she's ready to roll, Eddy," she said.

The mechanic wasn't easily sidetracked. "Thought he'd be back to Mimosa more often, what with New Mountain Farm and all. Thought for sure he'd call *you* plenty of times. Way you two looked at each other at the dance, thought for certain he'd be giving you a ring. What happened, Heather?''

Heather was determined not to reply to that direct question. "I've got to get back to Maggie's," was all she said.

Raif was gone. He'd gone off to Boston three weeks ago, just after the fair. She'd almost made another big mistake with Raif, but now she was back on track. She wasn't about to let memories and past mistakes clutter up her life. She was definitely not going to be one of those pathetic women who kept punishing themselves by falling in love with the same types of men.

Determinedly, Heather pulled Mehitabel up to the curb in front of Maggie's, edged past Thelma's old blue car and Lil's bicycle and hurried up the steps. At her approach the women called greetings and Maggie stuck her head around the kitchen door to demand, "You sure that old rattletrap's safe to drive?''

"It's going to have to be," Heather announced, and disappeared without answering the flurry of questions that floated out of the kitchen. Half an hour later, she'd showered off the grease and dirt of her morning's work and was standing in her bedroom when Maggie knocked on the door.

"Are you all right?" she asked.

Heather fumbled with the buttons on her shirt. "Damn," she muttered.

"Come on over here," Maggie ordered, then added as she closed the shirt, "You're as jumpy as a cat. You must be thinking of Raif again."

"Maggie, you're impossible. Why should I think about Raif?" Heather demanded irritably.

Maggie stepped back to watch Heather. "Because you've been missing him so much that you can hardly see straight," she then said.

"Don't be silly," Heather muttered.

"You two had something special going. I don't see why you're being so stubborn about it, sugar."

There was no use trying to lie to Maggie, Heather thought ruefully. She had the uncanny ability to get past what Heather was thinking and read her feelings. "You miss him, don't you?" Maggie was asking now.

Heather brushed back her hair and looked unseeingly into the mirror. "We're too different, Maggie."

"Sure. You're a woman, and he's a man."

"I didn't mean that and you know it. Our characters are too different. Our goals aren't the same. Besides, Raif is married to his work."

"And you think that he went back to Boston because he thought his work was more important than you," Maggie said. "That's why you blew up at him at the fair."

Heather surrendered. "Dammit, Maggie, I was worried about Raif. I was sure something had happened to him. And when he finally came, all he did was to talk about some stupid business deal. Sure I blew up.''

"No need to tell me that—half the folks at the fair heard you," Maggie responded. "You overreacted, sugar.''

"Maybe I did, but don't you see? Raif's work will always come first with him.''

"Like with Bill," Maggie murmured.

"It's *worse* with Raif because I couldn't bear to be second best in Raif's life—'' Heather broke off abruptly. She was sorry she'd let Maggie pressure her into talking about Raif. There was an undefinable ache in the middle of her breastbone, and she felt depressed.

"So you think life is perfect?" Maggie asked. Her voice was hard with an impatience that was so unlike her. "You and Raif got on fine together except for a few points that needed ironing out. But instead of taking the time to compromise, you tossed the whole relationship out the window. Do you think Sam and me had a perfect marriage?''

"*I* thought so. At least Sam was always considerate and kind.''

Maggie snorted. "That's all you know. Let me tell you, Sam and me had some fine old fights in the early days. One time right after we got married, I was so durn mad I threw an egg at him. Hit him, too.''

In spite of herself, Heather grinned. "No kidding? What did Sam do?''

"He walked out of the house and took off and was gone for hours. I was about to go after him, too, 'cept I was too proud. Then, when I was good and scared that something had happened to him, he came home

and told me he was sorry and we had a long, long
talk.'' Mággie rubbed the bony ridge of her nose and
sighed nostalgically. ''You know what compromise
really means?''

Heather rolled her eyes. ''Why do I have the feeling you're going to tell me?''

''Com-promise, get it? Two people get together and
say, 'Hey, you're not perfect but neither am I, so I'll
meet you halfway. Let's promise to grow and change
together.''' Maggie paused to draw breath. ''Sugar,
love is hard to come by. Don't you let something as
mean-spirited as pride stand in your way.'' She paused,
then claimed an urgent need to return to the kitchen,
and left.

Maggie's words clung like lint to Heather's mind.
Though she didn't want to admit it, Maggie was right
about one thing. She had acted like a self-righteous
ninny at the fair.

Raif had come late, but he *had* come. He'd done
what he could for Maggie with the cable networks,
too. But she'd been too furious to see that, and he'd
left for Boston before she'd had a chance to cool
down. She'd never had the chance to apologize for the
things she'd said.

Sam had always said that breathing deeply helped
clear the mind, and she tried it now. But her deep
breaths sounded like sighs, and the ache that had fas-
tened around her heart didn't go away. *All right, I give
up,* she told herself. She had to phone Raif and tell
him she was sorry. For a while they'd been important
to each other, and she didn't want Raif to remember
her as a hysterical vixen.

Heather walked slowly over to the phone, stood before it a long moment, then picked up the receiver and dialed the operator.

In a few moments, her call had been put through and a brisk female voice was saying, "Raifoods. How may I help you?"

Heather was pleased with the crisp way in which she explained that she'd like to speak to Mr. Cornell. "I'll connect you with his private secretary," the woman said.

There was a click, and in a few moments a pleasant voice asked what she could do to help.

Unfortunately, she couldn't. "Mr. Cornell? I'm so sorry, Miss Leigh. He's out of town on a business trip," Raif's private secretary informed her. "No, I'm not sure when he's expected to return. May I take a message?"

Heather said, "Thank you, no message," and hung up the phone. So, she told herself, that was that. No one could say she hadn't tried.

Of course Raif would be out somewhere on business. He was running true to form. By now, Mimosa must only mean New Mountain Farm to him and she, Heather, had probably become a distasteful memory. It wasn't that she'd expected anything else. So why did it feel as though someone had punched a hole in her heart?

A few minutes later, Heather wearily guided Mehitabel westward along Route 50. It had been a long day, and she felt drained. Which was why she'd decided to drive out to Skipper Nate's. The Homosassa would surely pick up her mood.

Heather parked Mehitabel near Skipper Nate's jetty, took her sketchbook from her portfolio and got out.

She wasn't going to think of Raif, but there he was in spite of her. Into Heather's mind popped the image of Raif leaning against the prow of the flat-bottomed boat.

Heather clenched her hands into fists. "Go away," she ordered. "Get out of my life."

But the memories would not retreat so tamely. Instead, her treacherous mind began to throw her more curves. She recalled the way Raif had run to save her from the attacking rooster, the way they'd played in the water at Pine Lagoon and how he had drawn her against his almost-naked, wet body and had looked down into her eyes.

A wind came out of nowhere and curled about her like a lover's hand. Heather breathed deeply and forced herself to concentrate on something else. On...on manatees.

Perhaps she'd sketch a couple swimming around— but that wouldn't be accurate, for manatees were solitary creatures. They only came together to mate.

She and Raif, too, had come together briefly, drawn by an inexplicable attraction to each other. Then, just in time, they'd retreated back to their own worlds.

The trouble was that her world seemed empty without Raif. Maggie had been right about that, but what Maggie didn't know was the degree of Heather's loneliness. When she'd broken off her engagement to Bill, she'd felt miserable, but she'd coped and become stronger. This parting from Raif was turning her inside out.

Everything she saw or touched, every sunset, each moonrise and evening star reminded her of Raif. Mehitabel reminded her of Raif. Going to New Mountain Farm to collect eggs and seeing George reminded her of Raif. Sketching brought him to mind. Everything had changed in her life and yet everything remained the same so that she seemed frozen in time, alone, without Raif.

"I've got to stop this," Heather muttered aloud.

"How long have you been talking to yourself?"

The deep voice wasn't real, Heather knew. It had to be her imagination. She'd been thinking of Raif so much that she was starting to hallucinate. Slowly she turned to confront the nothing she was sure to find, and instead saw him standing there.

He wasn't a figment of her imagination. He was very real and so was the rented car parked near Mehitabel. Raif was dressed in dark gray slacks that looked too warm for Florida and a pale blue shirt unbuttoned at the neck. The deep tan he'd acquired in Mimosa had faded, and he looked thinner and tired, but his eyes were the same. Green and a little wary, those eyes were regarding her intently.

"What are you doing here?" Heather gasped.

"Looking for you."

Raif's voice sounded brusque to his own ears, but he didn't know what to do about it. It wasn't how he'd meant to come across to Heather. He'd planned exactly what he wanted to say to her, but once he'd actually laid eyes on her, all his fine-sounding words had turned into mush.

"Looking for me?" Heather could have kicked herself for sounding like a wimpy echo. She made a rapid recovery and demanded, "Why?"

Her eyes weren't hazel, they were golden, Raif thought dazedly. "I needed to talk to you," he explained. "I guessed you'd be here."

How could he have guessed when she herself hadn't planned to come to Nate's until an hour ago? Tiny shock waves, set in motion by his presence, were starting to surge through Heather, and her mind began throwing out reasons to shield her heart.

No doubt he had some question about the drawings she'd already done for New Mountain Farm. That was it, of course. Business as usual for Raif—

He was saying, "I went to see Maggie first, and she told me you'd left without saying a word. I hoped you were headed here."

His voice had shed its original crispness and held instead the deep, soft notes she remembered. Under its layers of protection, Heather's heart gave a convulsive quiver.

"You see, I'm taking care of business." Raif watched her wince and damned himself for a fool. Hastily he amended, "I don't mean New Mountain Farm, either. I meant us."

She wanted to freeze him with a cool response, but all she could do was to parrot, "Us?"

"As in you and me. I didn't like the way we said goodbye—or didn't say goodbye. Heather, I'm sorry for the things I said."

He was so close to her that when she breathed, her lungs drew in the remembered scent of his cologne. The tone of his voice rubbed at something raw and tender inside her. With self-preservation on her mind, Heather backed away from him.

He followed. "I'm sorry for lousing up Maggie that day. I'm even more sorry for being too insensitive to understand why you were worried about me. If it helps any," he added, "I've kicked myself plenty."

They were too different. Their goals were different. Raif's work would always come first for him. With her defenses collapsing, Heather took another step back and reached the end of the jetty. *Between the devil and the deep blue river,* she thought.

Gently, Raif put his hands on her shoulders and drew her away from the edge of the jetty. "Heather, look at me. Please," he added.

Defiantly she met his eyes and then caught her breath. The expression on his face reminded her of how he'd looked the night of the dance.

"I've had a lot of time to think things through since I left Mimosa. Three weeks, four days, seven hours and twenty minutes, to be exact. At first I was too angry at you to realize what a fool I'd made of myself, and I almost convinced myself that my presence was crucial in Boston. But then I got smart."

He leaned down until his forehead almost touched hers. His hands were warm on her shoulders, and that familiar warmth was beginning to pulse down into her flesh. The last of Heather's bulwarks crumbled as he said, "I got smart when I saw how well my vice president and the head of my legal department were handling things. I suppose I'd known that deep down, but I convinced myself that my presence was crucial because I didn't want to face facts. I didn't want to admit how much you meant to me."

His voice died away in a moan of wind. Then he continued. "I didn't fly back to Boston in a hurry just because of Raifoods. At the dance I realized something that scared me. I found out that I was in love with you, Heather."

His voice was low, almost unsure. It wasn't Raif's usually confident voice. The low, uncertain tones seemed to reach into Heather's breast and capture her heart, and she spoke without thinking. "I've missed you so much."

"Sweetheart."

He didn't pull her into his arms as much as enfold her tenderly, as though she were infinitely precious to him. She felt the tremble in the hard-muscled arms that held her and said the words she'd said a hundred times in her heart. "I—I'm in love with you, too."

Now he drew her hard against him, and the words seemed to tumble out of him. "Thank God for that. Heather, I tried to forget you in Boston. I tried to immerse myself in my work, my world. But nothing was any good without you."

And wasn't that how it had been for her? Hadn't her life been dull and empty without him? But her thoughts were sheared away as his lips came down on hers. Their mouths touched, tasted, relearned the total reality of each other. Heather felt alive again, reborn. It was as if sunlight had shafted down into a dark place and transformed it into a glittering palace.

Then Raif drew a little apart from her. He said, "Sweetheart, listen to me. Raifoods is going places. Because of the interest shown in New Mountain Farm, I feel it's time to branch into the south. That's why

I've decided to acquire a subsidiary plant in Clearwater."

"Clearwater!" she exclaimed. "You mean, Clearwater, *Florida?*"

He nodded. "Since the initial months will be crucial to the subsidiary's success, I'm going to head it myself."

Raif was going to live in Clearwater, an hour's drive from Mimosa. Heather felt her head begin to whirl as she wondered, "What about your Boston-based company?"

"The way my top people handled things while I was gone proved that Boston Raifoods is in good hands. I'd have to fly back to Boston occasionally, of course, but it's only a three-and-a-half-hour trip." Raif paused to kiss the tip of Heather's nose. "Looks like you've been doing some acquiring yourself. There are a couple of new freckles here. Got to welcome them into the family."

So Raif was going to work in Clearwater *and* Boston. He'd have his hands full. But even if Raifoods took up most of his time, she wouldn't complain. That was what compromise meant, Heather thought happily. She could handle it as long as he didn't stop wanting to hold her, kiss her—

But he was talking again. "There's another thing we need to clear up. You were right on target when you said that I'd become obsessed with making Raifoods a success."

She winced. "Raif, I'm sorry about those things I said. I was mad. For a moment you reminded me of . . . of things that happened to me before and which had nothing to do with you. It was wrong, but—"

"No, you were right." His smile was tender. "My work is *not* my first love. I guess at first I wanted Raifoods to be a success for my dad's sake, and later it became a challenge that I enjoyed." He smoothed a curl away from Heather's forehead as he added, "My life didn't have any other direction then. As I said, I'm a lot smarter now."

He cradled her against his lean hardness. "What do you think of building in Clearwater? We need a house big enough for us and the children."

Heather started as if she'd been stung. "What are you talking about? What children?"

"Ours, of course. They come along, I've heard, after people get married."

Heather stared at him for a moment. Then her eyes narrowed. "Let's get this straight," she said slowly. "Do you mean that you want us to get married?"

He slid both arms around her and let his hands play over the silk of her blouse. "Will you?"

She didn't have to reply. Her eyes told him everything he needed to know. Raif's heart sang within him as he kissed her again. "I hope you don't believe in long engagements, sweetheart. I'm not a patient man."

Snuggling deeper into Raif's arms, Heather sighed in purest contentment.

"Let's go tell Maggie that she can start baking the wedding cake."

* * * * *

Silhouette romances are now available in stores at these convenient times each month.

Silhouette Desire
Silhouette Romance

These two series will be in stores on the 4th of every month.

Silhouette Intimate Moments
Silhouette Special Edition

New titles for these series will be in stores on the 16th of every month.

We hope this new schedule is convenient for you. With only two trips each month to your local bookseller, you will always be sure not to miss any of your favorite authors!

Happy reading!

Please note there may be slight variations in on-sale dates in your area due to differences in shipping and handling.

Take 4 bestselling love stories FREE

Plus get a FREE surprise gift!